I0684746

A LONE KID FROM TEXAS

A WESTERN NOVEL

BY

T. J. ROWDY

ISBN

978-0-9968449-1-8

First Edition

Published 2016

Dedication

This book is dedicated to my good friend of some thirty-five years, and the best Texan I ever met, Frank Toms.

Frank always said, "If you're happy, I'm happy for you".

This to me, is one of the best sayings ever. It is right up there with, "Do unto Others—"

Table of Contents

Chapter Number	Chapter Title	Page
Chapter 1	Poe	1
Chapter 2	The Ride	15
Chapter 3	The Men of Minersville	21
Chapter 4	Double Ought	27
Chapter 5	Appaloosa	35
Chapter 6	My horse, My Friend	45
Chapter 7	One on One	51
Chapter 8	Wolves	57
Chapter 9	Homeward Bound	65
Chapter 10	Bushwhack	73
Chapter 11	A Visit from Alice	81
Chapter 12	Convict Outlaws	87
Chapter 13	Hold Up	91
Chapter 14	Aftermath	95
Chapter 15	Hunted	105
Chapter 16	The Capture	119
Chapter 17	Horse Ranch	127
Chapter 18	Deputy Poe	131
Chapter 19	Scraps	139
Chapter 20	Bad News, Bad Men	147
Chapter 21	The Escape	155
Chapter 22	Caught 'Em	159
Chapter 23	The New Sheriff	165
Chapter 24	The Last Goodbye	171
Chapter 25	Twister	179
Chapter 26	Cactus Mac	183
Chapter 27	The Rescue	191

Acknowledgements

Written By: T. J. Rowdy

Edited and Formatted By: Dale L. Cox

Cover Image Usage: Creative Commons

Cover By: Dale L. Cox

Introduction

About the Author

It was only about eleven months ago, when I discovered that I have a talent for writing. I've played music for years, learned how to play several different instruments, and have always enjoyed creating music in all forms. I have been writing songs for over forty years, but I had never tried my hand at creative writing.

Since I'm now getting rather long in the tooth, so to speak, I decided to give it a try. I discovered that I not only like to write, but others, like what I write. I have a great imagination and a lot of passion for the characters that I create.

My first book is titled *Paradise Flats*. It is a somewhat lengthy western novel of life in the eighteen-hundreds. It is filled with lots of exciting western adventures. Paperback ISBN 978-0-9968449-0-1.

A Lone Kid from Texas is my second book. It is also a western novel of the same period. It is more focused on the personal character and strengths of a young cowboy, making his way in the Wild West. Paperback ISBN 978-0-9968449-1-8. Kindle ISBN 978-0-9968449-2-5.

I do feel there are a lot of people that will genuinely enjoy my work. I hope you are one of them.

T. J. Rowdy, Author

Preface

Wild West

A lot of people, may not know this, but the Wild West was a period of only about forty years, from 1860–1900. Back then, nearly every town west of the Mississippi, was wild and unruly. Most places only had one sheriff, or marshal, with perhaps a deputy to ensure the safety and wellbeing of the townsfolk. And, nearly everyone was armed with either a pistol, a rifle, or both, and sometimes, a large knife as well. Some would have a pistol on their side, and a smaller hideout elsewhere on their person, like a derringer in a vest pocket, or hidden in a boot. Ladies also carried derringers in their garters, or might have a razor or knife tucked away out of sight; but, nearly everyone was armed in one way or another, for their self-defense.

With lawbreakers, Indian attacks, diseases, and challenges from mother nature, it was a wonder that anyone survived at all. But, the strong did survive, and they helped shape the Wild West into what it eventually became, a decent, productive, healthy place to live, and to raise children. Yes, we are all indebted to our forefathers for enduring the trials and tribulations, of the by gone days of the Wild West.

It is in this setting, that *A Lone Kid From Texas,* (Poe Dievers) grew up, and met the challenges of the day, which shaped his personal character. This book shares his many experiences and relationships, as he navigated his way through this hostile environment. There are some touching moments as well as some action packed standoffs with the lawbreakers of the time.

I think you will enjoy his adventures.

T. J. Rowdy, Author

Poe

Chapter 1

Poe Dievers was seventeen when he was released from reform school, after serving a year for petty theft. But upon returning home, found that he no longer had one. It had been burned to the ground, because of a huge prairie fire. Due to a state wide drought, everything for miles around was dry as dust. So when lightening hit the prairie, boom, a huge fire was started, and the winds that drove the fire were nearly fifty miles per hour. So the fire raged across the prairie like a herd of frightened buffalo, destroying everything in its path. From desert trees to grasslands, to people's houses, nothing was spared. Driven by the high winds and ever searching for more and more fuel to feed it, the fire raced across the land like a giant hungry beast devouring everything in its path. The heat was so intense that it seared the lungs of Poe's father who had managed to get as far as the corral, before he died. His mother and siblings never got out of the house. The neighbors, and other town's folk had buried the remains of his family, and all Poe had left was four grave markers to indicate they had ever even been there.

He had sworn to himself that upon returning home he would tell his parents he had indeed learned his lesson, and would never steal again. But finding nothing but four markers in the ground, that didn't seem to matter much now. He was as alone as anyone could be, with no home, no family, and no means of support. He would walk back to what was left of the tiny town of Waycross, Texas, and try to find some work. He had already spent the entire morning walking here, and now he would have to walk the same distance back.

Plodding along the dusty road back to town, he heard cows, lots of cows coming in his direction. Then one of the men in charge of this herd, rode up and asked if he was lost.

"No sir I ain't lost, I know where I'm at. But I don't know exactly where I'm going on account of I lost my family and our house in that big fire we just had, and I'm trying to figger out what to do next."

"Well now boy, you ever punch cows?"

Poe, "No sir, but I reckin' I can learn, if you or someone will teach me."

"Well my name's Will Plunkett, and my boss, Mr. Waverly, I'm sure needs a few extra hands for this drive. So if you want to come along with me I'll introduce you to him. Here swing on up here." Lowering an arm and grabbing the boy the herdsman hauled him up onto his horse behind him.

Riding up to the cowboy camp, Poe swung down and stood waiting to be introduced to the boss of the trail herd.

Will, "Mr. Waverly, I found this kid out yonder a walking, and he needs a job. He lost his folks and all to that big fire we had."

"Is that so boy?" asked Waverly.

Poe, "Yes sir, I was in the reform school when it happened, and I just come here to see my folk's grave."

Waverly "What were you in for boy?"

"I stole some money off a drunk man, and they sent me up for it. But I promised my pa before I got out that I'd never do that again. And, I surely won't, no matter what, on account of I promised him."

Waverly, "Well seein' as how you got no place to go, and I need more men to finish this drive, you're hired on at half pay until you get the hang of herding these ornery critters. I figure it shouldn't take you more than a couple of weeks, and then you'll get a dollar a day like everybody else. That seem fair to you?"

Poe, "Yes sir. Thank you Mr. Waverly."

"Tell Curly, that's our cook, that I said to feed you, and I'll get one of the boys to cut you out a horse from the remuda; welcome to the drive."

Now the boy had a place to be, and a job to do, and most of all he had a readymade family of cowpunchers, men who like himself, either had no ties to anyone, or any particular place to go. Before the herd got to its destination, he would experience many exciting things, two Indian attacks, an attempt by rustlers to steal the herd, a huge wind storm, and the loss of one cowboy to drowning, all on this one cattle drive to Ellensberg, Kansas, their final destination.

It took more than three months to get there, but they had finally arrived in Ellensberg with three quarters of the herd, about twenty-seven hundred cows. He was no longer a boy fresh out of reform school, but a man of eighteen and now a cowboy. He had shot and killed an Indian during one of the attacks on the drive, had learned how to ride a horse in all sorts of weather, and held his own in a scuffle with another drover. Two things he would purchase with some of his pay was his own six-gun, and eventually a horse of his own. But first with the prompting of several other herdsmen, he would get his first taste of whiskey and women. Like several other saloons in the old west, the Boot Heal Saloon was a place frequented by all or most of the cowhands upon their arrival in town.

"Howdy Madge, come here and give me a kiss," said Will, when several of them entered the bar.

Madge, "Why you, you old outlaw? I think I'd rather kiss this young fella right here." With that Madge threw her arms around Poe and kissed him on the lips smack! "How's that cowboy?" she asked.

Poe's face reddened, with embarrassment. He had never been kissed by a woman before, except of course his mother. Poe "Um a that were fine, I reckin'."

Madge, "Just fine? Well let me do it again and maybe I kin make it better this time." Madge grabbed Poe by the back of his head and kissed him for several seconds, and then let go. The lad's eyes opened wide and he let out a Yahoo!

Madge, "That's what I wanted to hear. Welcome to Ellensberg!"

Then there was a lot of drinking, and dancing, and merriment enjoyed by all. The next morning, Poe was experiencing his first hangover. With his head pounding like a drum, he went to the chuck wagon to ask Curly the cook what if anything could be done for his new predicament.

Curly, "You look like you been dragged through a knothole boy, here have some coffee, and if you can manage some food, that will help some too."

Poe, "If this is what happens when a body drinks, I ain't never gonna drink again."

Curly, "Oh, if I had a nickel every time I heard that, I'd be one rich hombre. You drink that coffee and it'll fetch you around afore long."

Poe, "Thanks Curly."

Curly, "You're welcome boy. Can I give you some good advice?"

Poe, "Sure Curly, what's that?"

Curly, "The next time you decide to drink, either stick to beer, or don't have more than one whiskey an hour, that way you can still function."

Poe, "I'll remember that, thanks."

Mr. Waverly, "Well Poe, how was your first trip going to see the elephant?"

Poe, "Going to see the what?"

Waverly, "Oh, that's what we call it. We're heading back to Texas tomorrow, you going with us?"

Poe, "No offense Mr. Waverly, but I don't know for sure whether or not I'm cut out to be a cowpuncher er not."

Waverly, "Well now son, you did alright for your first drive, and this kind of life ain't made for everyone. But if next spring you want to

4

come along with us, you're welcome to."

"Thanks Mr. Waverly, I'll consider it next spring."

"OK boy, you take care of yourself, you hear?"

"Yes, sir." Poe was alone again, but now he was a man, and thanks to Will's advice, had put most of his pay in his boot, so he wouldn't be flat broke after a night in town. He thanked his lucky stars for that. Having purchased a colt peacemaker pistol, along with a belt and holster and a box of shells, now all he really needed was a good horse. Not just any horse, but a horse that he could ride for a long way without tiring, wasn't too hard to handle, but still had spirit. He would go to the livery and see what was available.

Not seeing anything to his liking he returned to the saloon, to see if he could find some information on where else to go to buy one. Upon entering the saloon, Madge saw him and again came over to kiss him, only this time he waited and when she was within reach, grabbed her and kissed her on the lips and spanked her on the rump. "Hi ya darling," said Poe.

Madge, "You sure learn fast kid. But, you're gonna need a lot more practice to be a really good kisser."

Poe, "I'll get by. Can I have a beer?"

Madge, "Sure thing honey, and I want to introduce you to somebody I think you'll cotton to. Lisa, come on over here; I got someone I want you to meet."

Lisa was a twenty year-old nicely built woman with sandy brown hair, and big blue eyes, not gorgeous but not bad to look at either. She also had a Texas drawl that sounded fine to him. Lisa, "Howdy boy, you here to see the elephant?"

Poe, "First off, I ain't no boy and I already seen that elephant yesterday, and don't think I'd care to visit again."

"Smart boy," said Lisa.

Poe, "I told you, I ain't no boy. I just finished a trail drive all the way from Texas to here, with two thousand seven hundred and two cows, and I'm full grown. So I'm a man now."

Lisa, "I guess I can't argue that, you looking for some company Mr. er a?"

"Mr. Dievers; my names Poe Dievers, and maybe after a bit I might be inclined to spend some time with you, but right now I'm trying to find me a good horse. I thought maybe I could get a lead on one here."

Lisa, "Oh I see, well cowboy after you find your horse you come on back and see me, you hear."

Poe leans over and gently kissed her on the cheek, "I'll do that." Fifteen minutes later, not having any good leads on where to go to purchase a good horse, Poe decided to get a room at the hotel. After acquiring a room, he went upstairs, put his gun belt on the chair next to the bed, laid down staring at the ceiling and fell fast asleep. When he awakened four hours later, it was dark. Not knowing the exact time, Poe made a mental note to purchase a pocket watch the next time he went to the general store.

He decided to wait a while to find a really good mount, instead of just buying what was available, after all a horse was the single most important item that any cowboy would ever own. A pistol could save your life, if you didn't get shot, or run out of bullets first. But a horse could oft times get you out of trouble, quicker than you got into it. Besides, although he had a six-gun, and ammunition, he was going need a lot of practice with it before he could trust the weapon as much as he trusted his ability to ride away from any perceived danger. He would set aside a couple of hours every day to practice, once he checked with the sheriff about when and where it was lawful to do this. He also needed to find some steady work, but this was not the time or place to do either one so, he would go back to the saloon and see Lisa again.

Upon entering The Boot Heel Saloon, he saw Lisa engaged in conversation with one or more men seated at the bar. He would get a beer and wait for her to see him, so as not to seem too anxious. Within a few minutes he felt sultry hands gently rubbing his back and turning around saw Lisa grinning at him. "Howdy Poe, you come back a looking for me?"

Poe, "Why, were you expecting me?"

Lisa coyly, "Maybe; I figured you'd be back in here, only I didn't know whether it'd be tonight or not. You looking to spend a little time with me upstairs?"

Poe, "I guess that depends on what we're gonna do, and what it's gonna cost me."

"Well, if'n you got a dollar to spend, and you're of mind to spend it on me, then I'll show you the rest of me, only without no clothes on."

Poe, "Oh! I reckin' that'd be fine, only I gotta tell you that I ain't never seen a woman naked before, and I ain't at all sure of what I'm supposed to do."

Lisa, "That's OK honey, I'll be gentle with you, and since this is your first time, I'll do my very best to see that you get your dollar's worth. You go on and finish your beer, and I'll be right back." Five minutes later the two were upstairs, and Lisa was disrobing a little at a time. With her breasts exposed, and shaking her hair out, she looked beautiful. Lisa, "Come on now cowboy, you can't get nothin' done with your clothes on. Take them duds off."

Feeling slightly embarrassed, and not wanting to take his eyes off her firm young body, Poe fumbled with the buttons on his shirt, and britches. Lisa, "Here let me help you with those." Now naked, she threw her arms around him, and kissing him passionately; she pulled him onto the bed. The two lovers explored each other's naked bodies, and ended up covered in sweat and panting on the bed. Lisa, "Whew! You sure you never did this before?"

Poe, "No ma'am, I surely woulda remembered doing that!"

Lisa, "I got to tell ya honey, if this really WAS your first time, I can't wait to you get practiced up. You kin come and see me anytime you've a mind to, and I don't say that to everyone."

"Are we done now?" asked Poe.

Lisa, "Usually we would be, but if you wanna go again that's fine by me, and I ain't gonna charge you nothing extra." Forty minutes later the two were dressing and coming down the stairs, with the other girls watching.

Cindy, "Damn Lis, I thought you-uns turned in early, you been up there for quite a spell." Lisa didn't respond, but smiled and went to the bar and ordered a shot.

Not knowing what to do next, Poe walked over to the bar and ordered a beer. "I think I'm going to like this place," he said. Now he knew about women, and whiskey, but he still needed to practice shooting, and find some decent work. Not that herding cows was not decent, it was good honest work, just not very glamorous for a young man out to find himself a place in the world. He wasn't sure what he wanted to do to make a living, but it wasn't herding cows for the rest of his life. Besides he had heard that once the railroads were extended southward into Texas that driving cows to market would not be necessary. So he would find some other way to make a living.

Maybe the stage line was in need of someone like him. He would go to the restaurant, have some breakfast, and then check to see. He walked over to Bell's place, that was the name of the town's one and only eating establishment, and ordered a bacon and eggs breakfast. While eating he listened for any opportunity for work. He still had most of his pay from the cattle drive, but that wasn't going to last forever. He had enough to last a month or so, but then he still needed a good horse, and a really good horse wasn't going to be cheap. After being told that the stage line was not hiring, he tried the freight lines.

"Morning," said Poe. "I'm Poe Dievers, and I'm looking for work, would there be anything around here you might need a hand with?"

"Howdy young fella, my name's Bert Thomson and I do in fact need a man to help with the loading and unloading, from time to time, but nothing on a permanent basis. I pay two bits a wagon, if that's agreeable to you. We don't get a wagon load every day, but some days we might have three or four. You do four wagons, that's a dollar. Same as you'd get on a trail drive only it don't take as long to earn it."

Poe, "How'd you know I was a cowpuncher?"

Bert, "It's a small town. The town, a lota times, gains a new member, or two after every trail drive. A cowboy gets drunk and breaks the law goes to jail for a spell, and can't make the trip back, or only makes one drive, and decides that he don't want to do that kind of work no more, like you. Like I said it's a small town, and some folks just can't stand not knowing everything about a new person in town. So you're likely to get a lot of questions about you from people you ain't never even met before, especially the women folk. Lord do they like to gossip."

Poe, "I see, I will have to make a point of not talking to them."

"Oh no, you don't want to do that, 'cause if you don't talk to them, 'bout nothin'. They'll make up stories about you that ain't true."

Poe, "Why would they do that?"

Bert, "Just 'cause they ain't got nothing going on in their own lives, worth talking 'bout. So they gossip about everybody else. It's kinda sad really."

Poe, "It surely is."

Bert, "Anyway, I got a wagon load of freight coming in around four o'clock, and if you want to make two bits, be here at four."

Poe, "I'll be here." Poe said goodbye to Mr. Thomson and went to the Boot Heel to have a beer an see Lisa.

"Howdy Poe," said Wallace the bartender, "a beer?"

Poe, "Sure thing. Where's Lisa?" Poe asked.

Wallace, "Oh, she don't start till five."

Poe was minding his own business sipping at his beer, when a cowboy bumped into him and spilled his beer, and then turned back to his friends without even saying excuse me.

Poe, "Hey there cowboy, you just spilled my beer."

Cowboy, "So what! Buy another one."

"The least you could do is say excuse me."

Cowboy, "To who, you!"

Poe, "Yeah to me. For all I know you did that on purpose."

Cowboy, "So what if I did, what are you going to do about it?"

Poe, "I reckin' I'll have an apology from you."

Cowboy, "Is that so. I don't apologize to nobody, fer nothing, especially a pup like you."

Poe made the mistake of starting to reach for his colt, when the man drew and cocked his pistol, and aimed it at his face, but did not pull the trigger. Poe stood frozen knowing he could have been killed, had the man wanted him dead.

The cowboy said, "You're lucky kid, I generally shoot someone for doing that. But I ain't of a mind to even talk to a law dog right now. So go on and get." With that said, he grabbed Poe by the collar and hurled him toward the doors.

Poe was incensed, and humiliated but knew he was over matched, so he just left for his hotel room. Once back in his room, Poe was running the incident over in his mind, and feeling very small as a man. He would make a concerted effort to practice the fast draw with his colt every day in his room, and practice shooting at targets on the outskirts of town whenever he could. That would be his focus for the next several days, weeks or months, until he felt he was ready. One thing he was sure about, was that nothing like that would ever happen to him again. He would get good at drawing and firing, and hitting whatever he aimed at. He still had an hour before work so first he would go buy another box of shells, and begin today.

As soon as he finished the first wagon, another had arrived, he was asked if he could unload that one as well. Poe, "Sure thing Mr. Thomson, I ain't got nothing pressing to do." He was already limbered up from unloading the first wagon, and the second one he managed to unload in half the time.

"By God you're a real rip snorter when it comes to unloadin' boy. Do you know, that were the fastest unloading I ever had, and I'm going bump your pay up to four bits a wagon load."

Poe, "Gee thanks, Mr. Thomson."

"No, thank you boy; I mean it. I timed you same as I've timed everybody else that ever did this job fer me, and you were five minutes faster than the fastest man I ever hired. I know, 'cause I timed ever one of 'em."

Poe, "I don't know what to say, 'cept thanks."

"You come here at first light in the mornin', and you kin load the outgoing freight, and if you're as fast at loading as you are unloading, well then, I might just have to hire you on full time. Just do me a favor and don't get yerself hurt. I'm going need you in the next few weeks. Here's yer pay."

"Mr. Thomson, you done give me too much money, here."

"An and honest man to boot. No son, I meant to give you that. You earned every cent. Now you go and see that gal at the Boot Heel, and I'll see you in the morning."

Poe, "How'd you know 'bout Lisa?"

Bert, "Like I said, it's a small town."

Feeling more manly, Poe walked in to the Boot Heel, but was

secretly praying that the man that had embarrassed him would not be there. He wasn't.

Lisa walked up and kissed him and said, "Hiya Poe, you lookin' fer me?"

Poe, "Yes, but I wasn't sure whether er not I should, on account of what happened earlier. I didn't know if you'd want to see me."

Lisa, "Of course I do, I'm just glad that gunfighter didn't kill you."

"Gunfighter?"

"Yeah, that hombre is a hired gun, and they say that he's killed lots of men in gun fights, that's how come he ain't here now, on account of the sheriff told him to leave town."

Poe, "Oh, I didn't know that."

Lisa, "In case you're interested, his name is Bad Bob. I don't figger he'll be back in here any time soon, so you-uns don't have to fret over him none."

Poe, "You think we could get a table and talk for a bit. I'd like to get to know you better, if you've a mind to do that."

Lisa, "Sure thing sugar, let's set over yonder by the winda."

Poe and Lisa had been sitting and talking for a half an hour when all at once a fist fight broke out at the poker table. "You're a cheatin'! You got that card off'n the bottom of the deck, and I'm going kill you!"

"No you're not! both of you just hold it right there," said the sheriff, who had just walked in.

"Sheriff, he's been a cheatin'."

"Oh no I didn't; you're just a sore loser, is all."

"No matter," said the sheriff, "the game's over, both of you get out,

and come back later when you can behave yourselves, now git."
The sheriff's name was Farley Higgins. He was a man in his
thirties, average build, and average height, but had the eyes of a
man that had seen or done a lot of troubling things in his life, a real
no nonsense kind of lawman.

Farley, "You must be Poe, the new kid. I heard what happened
earlier, and I'm glad to see that you weren't foolish enough to come
back in here looking for retribution. That man that braced you was
a hired killer."

Poe, "Yeah I heard, I reckin' I'm lucky."

Farley, "More like you got good sense. Men like him get by with
killin' guys like you that don't have any. I've heard some good
things about you from some of the folks in town. You plannin' on
stayin' here awhile?"

Poe, "I suppose so, I don't have any place to be. I lost my folks in
that big prairie fire, and then I got a job pushing cattle to here, and
don't have any reason to leave, right off."

Farley, "You just do your work, don't get into no trouble and you'll
do fine."

Lisa, "You wanna go upstairs, Poe."

Poe, "Well I just made a dollar today and I haven't spent but fifty
cents, so I reckin' we could do that." The next morning Poe was up
early and on the job, loading the freight wagon for the day's
deliveries. Bert asked him if he would like to go with the driver as
a shotgun rider.

Poe, "To tell you the truth, I never even fired a shotgun before,
don't you need someone with a bit more experience?"

"Normally yes, but I think you can handle it; besides, there usually
isn't anything at all happens that you'll need to shoot anybody."

Poe, "OK, if you think it'll be alright, I'll go."

A Lone Kid From Texas   T. J. Rowdy

"This is your driver; his name is Ted Lampsin. Ted this is Poe."

Ted, "Howdy, you-uns ready?"

Poe, "Yeah I reckin'."

Ted hands him a double barrel shotgun, and hollers at the horses,
"Git up there!"

The Ride

Chapter 2

Poe and Ted had ridden for about ten miles, when Ted said, "Kid, did I hear you say that you never fired a shotgun afore?"

Poe, "Yes sir, never; my pa had one but he never let us even touch it. He said he would show us how to use it when we were older, and then he died in the fire. So I never got to learn."

"Then I reckin' I'll have to teach ya. Climb down and we'll have a short lesson. First off, always know whether or not it's loaded, and weather you got both barrels available, or just one. Go on and check it, like this." Ted takes the shotgun and breaks it open, "See two shells in it. But you see that little round spot in the center?"

Poe, "Yes."

"If it had been fired already, that little round spot would have a dent right smack dab in the center of it. Watch this." Ted takes the weapon and aims at a scrub oak and pulls the trigger. BOOM! "Now check it."

Poe breaks it open like Ted had showed him and there in the center was a small indentation.

"That is where the firing pin hit the blasting cap inside the shell, causing the explosion, and propelling the pellets or a deer slug outward, if that's what you loaded it with."

"A deer slug?"

Ted, "Yes, a deer slug. It's a big ol' ball they put in there instead of pellets. It's for big game like deer, or elk. But most folks use a rifle to hunt deer with anyway, so you need-unt worry too much 'bout that. Now a shot gun has a larger killing radius, than a rifle or a pistol, and it's downright deadly at close range. You shoot a man with a pistol, or even a rifle you may not kill him, depending on where he gets shot. But a shotgun full of double ought buckshot at close range, is almost a certainty. Here pick out a target and have at er."

Poe looks around and sees a cholla and says, "How 'bout that?" pointing to the cactus.

Ted, "OK, let er rip." BOOM! The buck shot shattered the upper part of the cactus. "Wow," said Poe, "that really tears up whatever it hits."

Ted, "Yep, that's why most men back off when it comes to facing down a shotgun. It's kinda hard to miss anyone at close range with one of these. You point this here shotgun at somebody, and I guarantee he'll be paying attention to everything you do and say, if'n he has any sense that is. Another thing, don't go pointing it at anybody unless you plan on using it. We probably won't have no 'cause to use it, but then you never know. You try and get into the habit of watching behind us, so we won't have no surprises, OK?"

Poe, "Sure thing Ted, I'll keep my eyes peeled. Shouldn't we get to moving?"

Ted, "Yeah I reckin'. Climb back up here, and we'll get on down the trail."

"Oh, by the way Ted, where we going anyway?"

Ted, "We're headin' for a mining camp, about a day's ride from Timinsville."

Poe, "Two days?"

Ted, "Yep, we should be there by dark, why you got an appointment er something?"

Poe, "No, I just wondered if we were going to have time to eat supper before we turn in, and maybe a night cap."

Ted, "And, check out the town's females?"

Poe, "I can look what's for sale; don't mean I gotta buy something."

Ted, "Right." That night, the men had dinner at the diner, and then got rooms at the hotel. Then they decided that since it was still fairly early, they would get a drink at the local watering hole. The Silver Cup Saloon was pretty much like every other saloon in the Old West, with the usual assortment of libations, beer, whiskey, brandy, wine, and sarsaparilla. Some saloons, like this one, even had the makings for sandwiches, cheese, sliced meat, and maybe a pickle, an the ever popular boiled egg, or sometimes a pickled egg. And, nearly every saloon, had women. For most men, this was as big an attraction, as the alcohol.

Timinsville, Kansas had a population of eight hundred and thirty-four people, full of subsistence farmers, and ranchers, and sprinkled with a few prospectors, buffalo hunters, and tradesmen. Usually, there was one doctor, a mayor, a sheriff, or marshal, a deputy or two, an undertaker, barber, and telegraph operator. Oft times one person would have two or more functions. Like the guy who cut your hair one morning, was the same guy that buried you after getting yourself killed in a gunfight two days later. There were many dual purpose people.

Such a person, was Katie Udall, a saloon girl at night, and a dress maker, and seamstress during the day. Katie was one of those tireless people that it seemed could go on working for hours after everyone else had gone home. She would run the dress shop from Monday till Saturday [her biggest day of the week] and then go to the saloon until midnight, sleep for three or four hours, and go back to the dress shop. Except on Sunday, when she would sleep in till eight o'clock, attend church at ten, and spend the rest of the day drawing designs for new dresses. Katie was a strong willed, independent, attractive, intelligent woman in her mid to late twenties with a no nonsense attitude about men. If she wanted to have a drink with someone she would, and if she didn't she wouldn't, the same with dancing, conversation or even serving drinks. If you acted crude or boorish, she would simply ignore you.

That's the way she was, and nobody was going to change her.

She introduced herself to Ted and Poe, and decided that they were not of the kind that would try to induce her to do something she wasn't fond of. So she came over and sat down with them, at the bar. "Howdy fellas, how you all doing this evening?"

"Just dandy ma'am, and you?" said Ted.

"Oh, I'm about the same as always, I reckin'. Can I get you boys another beer?"

Ted, "Sure I'll have one more, what about you Poe?"

Poe, "No thanks, I think I'm gonna head for the hotel and turn in. I'll see you in the morning."

"OK, good night Poe."

Katie returned with Ted's beer but before she could reseat herself, was grabbed by the arm by an obnoxious man with a pocked face, and a rude disposition. "Come here gal an give me a kiss."

Katie slapped the man in the face and said, "You just hold on there mister! I'm no side of beef you can push around, let go of me."

The man 's name was Baxter Hargrove, a medium sized man, sporting two pistols and a large knife. Baxter, "I ain't used to being told by no gal. Now if you want to stay pretty, you had better change your tune, or I might have to cut that pretty face of yours." With that said he pulled the large Bowie knife from its scabbard and held it menacingly a foot away from Katie's face. Ted flew off his barstool and grabbed the man's wrist that held the knife and kneed him in the crotch with his right knee, followed by a hard punch in the face, with an overhand left, knocking him to the floor. This action caused Baxter to drop the knife, but he reached for his pistol and Ted did the same. Both men fired BLAM BLAM. Baxter's bullet hit Ted in the chest and he died almost instantly. While Ted's bullet got Baxter in the left thigh. Katie screamed and the whole bar became a mass of noise and confusion.

Poe learned of the untimely death of his friend the next morning, when the sheriff knocked on the door of his room. Knock knock knock. Poe, "Just a minute. Uh, good morning. You must be the sheriff. What can I do for the law this morning?"

Sheriff, "Sit down son, I've got some bad news for you."

Poe sat down on the bed, "OK, what?"

"Well boy, I'm afraid your friend, the guy you came here with, well he's dead; he got shot in a gun fight last night in the saloon."

Poe, "No, no, no. Who done it?"

Sheriff, "A man name of Hargrove, a Baxter Hargrove, nobody special just a drifter. Him and your friend, shot each other last night in the saloon over a woman."

Poe, "You sure about that, Sheriff?"

Sheriff, "That's what I was told, you can go and talk to Katie if you'd like. I'm sorry for the loss of your friend. Katie explained that Ted was just trying to be the gentleman that he was, and paid for it with his life."

"Well, I reckin' I'll have to head on back to Ellensberg, on account of this was my first trip and I don't know how to get to that mining camp."

Over hearing the boy say mining camp, a miner stranded because he was too drunk to stay in the wagon, and thereby missed his ride back to the camp said he would show Poe the way to go, if he could ride along with him, back to the mining camp where Poe needed to deliver the wagon load of goods. The miners name was Donald Barton. "Well Mr. Barton, you got a deal. You show me the way, and I'll give you a ride."

Donald, "Great, I'll sure show them fellers that said I'd lose my claim if'n I didn't make it back, ha, ha." So with a new passenger, Poe was once again on his way, to his destination.

* * *

The Men of Minersville

Chapter 3

Poe could smell the camp long before he got there. The stench was suffocating, with more than two dozen men working up a sweat every day, and none of them had bathed in God knows how long. The smell was not to be believed, but all the men there were all miners, and were all in the same place, at the same time, doing the exact same thing, digging for gold. A couple of miners had actually found a little gold. Thus the reason that they and the rest of them kept right on digging. Day in and day out, they were digging in the dirt with picks and shovels, breaking boulders into rocks, and then breaking the rocks into smaller rocks. Some of these men would spend all day bending over in the stream and panning for gold, all of them constantly searching for that one good strike that would make them wealthy.

Their diet was the three b's: biscuits, beans, and sometimes, usually only a day or two of bacon. They drank coffee in the morning and whiskey at night, all day every day, they were fighting mother nature for her well-hidden bounty. But these men had an unwritten code of conduct. No one steals from anyone, and disputes were generally settled with their fists, unless there was a killing, then a make shift court was held, and the transgressor was dealt with. If you were found guilty then you would be hanged, right then and there, and the body was left to hang for a while, usually only a day or two, as a reminder. This was the first thing Poe saw when he pulled into camp with the wagon load of supplies.

When the supplies were unloaded, Poe discovered that at least a third of his load was dynamite. "Well I'll be," said Poe. "I didn't know we were hauling dynamite; else I might not have made this trip. I'll be sure to check next time, if I decide to do this again." Donald explained to everyone that Ted had been killed in a gunfight, by the last man they had ousted from their camp for being too unsavory for any of them to stand. He was breaking their unwritten code of conduct. Poe was delighted to find that when it came to unloading the goods from the wagon, that he didn't have to lift a finger, as all had chipped in and had everything out of the wagon before he could spit, which saved him a lot of sweat, as the temperature was already in the high eighties. These were some tough men indeed. Poe was introduced to a lot of them, before he departed for home.

With the horses being rested, and an empty wagon, he would make the trip back in way less time, even after he stopped in Timinsville, for a cold beer and maybe get the chance to talk with the lovely Katie one more time. He pulled the wagon up in front of the Silver Cup Saloon, got down and went inside. But to his dismay, there was the same man that had shot and killed his friend, sitting at the bar. Which he had not seen before, as he left town while this man was at the doctors being treated for his wound. Luckily, Katie was there and saw him before anyone could tell him of this. Katie, "Hiya sugar; you have a nice trip?"

Poe, "Well thanks to my last minute passenger, I found it OK. Now I guess I can find my way back there. How you been?"

Katie, "Me, oh 'bout the same, I reckin'. Poe, can I give you some sound advice?"

Poe, "Sure what's that?"

"Finish your beer an git."

Poe, "But I just got here and was hoping to maybe buy you a beer and sit for a spell."

Katie, "I didn't want to be the one to tell you this but, you see that guy there at the bar?"

Poe, "Yeah."

Katie, "That's the same man that killed your friend."

Poe felt his muscles tense. Poe, "How come he ain't in jail?"

Katie, "'Cause they said it was self-defense; your friend did pull his pistol too."

Poe, "I didn't know him long but I don't think he would of shot anyone without a good cause."

Katie, "The sheriff said he couldn't charge him with nothing. But seeing as how he don't know you were his partner, I'd suggest you git on back home."

Poe, "You're probably right, I'll go."

Just when he thought he was going to get out without a confrontation, Baxter stopped him. "Hey kid, I'm the one that shot your friend and I been waiting for you."

Poe, "I don't even know you mister, and I don't want no trouble."

Baxter, "Oh, you're a coward! I shoulda known, you being that other coward's friend an all."

Poe, starting to become incensed at this, said, "Look you, my friend weren't no coward, and I ain't neither. Why don't you just go your way, and I'll go mine."

Baxter, "You're a coward! Put on a gun, prove you're not yella."

"That's enough Baxter get out," said the sheriff. "I told you not to cause no more trouble. So that's it. Get your ass out of here; matter of fact, get out of my town all together! You ain't welcome here."

"Why you," said Baxter and started to pull his pistol, but the sheriff, already for him, had his pistol in hand and cocked and aiming it at his head.

Sheriff, "Go on pull that hogleg and see what happens." Baxter knew he was effectively disrupted and took his hand away from his pistol. Baxter, "I'll leave, but I'll be seeing you again," pointing to Poe.

23

Poe thanked the sheriff for his quick intervention, and relaxed a bit. Then the sheriff introduced himself, "I been told your name's Poe, that right?"

Poe, "Yes sir."

"I'm Sheriff Winters, Alvin Winters, and I think you had better stay here for a spell, on account of that fella's going be expectin' you to ride past him on your way home, and like as not, he'll shoot you."

Poe, "In cold blood! how can that happen?"

Alvin, "Easy, out there on the prairie's a no man's land and if there ain't no witnesses, then there ain't no crime. You follow?"

Poe, "I see, but I can't stay here forever. I got to be back on account of it's my job."

"I tell you what young fella, I'll send a wire to your sheriff and tell him I have detained you as a material witness in a murder trial, and you won't be in no trouble. You see I figure that fellas gonna camp right side of the road to intercept you on your way back home. But I'm betting he won't stay there more than an few hours, because of the heat, and there ain't nothing out there 'cept lots of rattlers and lizards and a whole lot of sun. So I don't fancy him stayin there, waitin' for too long a time. In fact, I'll bet you he won't wait more than a couple of hours. But just so you're safe, why don't you spend the night here, and then leave come first light. How'd that be?"

Poe, "OK, I reckin'; thanks for sending that wire, and explaining to my boss."

Winters, "You're welcome. You two have fun, I'll be around later; bye now."

"Bye Sheriff," said Poe and Katie. Poe, "I guess I'll have to tell the hotel I'm staying another night."

Katie, "Not necessarily, you could maybe spend the night with me; that is, if you really wanted to?"

"I er, that is, I um, sure, I reckin'."

Katie, "You reckin'; you don't sound too sure, don't you like me?"

Poe, "Oh yes ma'am, I do like you a lot, but I don't know whether I got enough money for, er that is to say, I um—"

Katie interrupts him and gives him a big kiss, causing him to blush. Katie, "Good, it's settled you spend the night with me and it ain't gonna cost you nothing. I figure that's the least this town can do seein' as how you lost your friend here. Let's have a couple more beers and then we'll go on upstairs."

After spending the evening in the embrace of this soft, sexy, warm wonderful woman, Poe felt as if he could take on the world. "I gotta tell you Katie, last night was the best night of my whole life, and just the thought of seeing you again is gonna make that dusty trip here more than worth it."

Katie, "Well, thank you Poe, and I'd have to say that I'll be looking forward to seeing you again, the sooner the better, but you best be leaving before it gets too hot out."

With that, Poe leaned over and gave her a goodbye kiss. "See you soon, Katie."

"Bye Poe."

He readied the wagon and horses and climbed aboard the wagon and gently whipped the horses. They responded and away he went out of town. Now he was alone on the trail, just him and the team of horses, but with a new found sense of purpose. Now he had more reason than ever to make this trip, and since Ted's death, he would be the best candidate to come here again. All he really had any worry about, was Baxter. But it seemed the sheriff had been right about Baxter not waiting to ambush him. He searched the terrain for signs of a rider and saw nothing out of place. Good a nice quiet trip back and that was fine by him.

* * *

Double Ought

Chapter 4

Once Poe arrived back in Ellensberg, he was relieved to find that not only was he not in any trouble for being late getting there, but he was heralded by his boss Mr. Thompson for not getting himself killed as well. "You did just fine boy," said Mr. Thompson. "I surely hated to lose Ted, but at least, you had sense enough to stay clear of the same trouble."

"To tell you the truth Mr. Thompson, that thar hombre wanted to kill me too, but the sheriff stopped him and threw him out of town, and don't you worry, I'm going to keep a sharp eye out for him in the future. He won't ever catch me unaware, that's a promise." I know for a fact that Sheriff Winters don't like that man much, and he'd be in real trouble if he were to try anything at that mining camp. All them fellas was real glad to see me, and they all liked Ted. So I figure the only time he can bother me is out on the trail, going there or coming back, and he better have a horse that's fast enough to outrun buckshot, if'n he wants to take me on the trail."

"Sounds like you grew up some on that trip."

Poe, "I don't see that I had any say in the matter at all. I was just trying to do my job, is all."

"You did fine son," said Mr. Thompson. "Oh by the way, here's your pay, and that gal Lisa came by here asking for you, so you might want to go by the saloon and say howdy to her."

"Yeah, I'll do that thanks."

Lisa saw him before he got to the door, and ambushed him with a kiss, smack! "Hiya handsome, welcome back."

"Hi Lisa; you miss me?"

Lisa, "I surely did. I heared you had some trouble on yer trip that so?"

Poe, "A little, I reckin'."

Lisa, "A little, didn't Ted get hisself killed?"

Poe, "Well yes, he did, but that ain't gonna happen to me, on account of I know who and what to look for now, and that's all the edge I'm gonna need. He won't ever catch me unaware or sleepin', and if he pushes me I'll be ablieged to introduce him to two barrels of double ought buckshot. He tries anything out on the trail, and it's adios for him. I don't plan on doing nothin' else but work, sleep, and practice shooting, from now on."

Lisa, "Nothing else?"

Poe, "I said sleeping too."

Lisa, "But, you didn't say where you-uns was going to sleep, did ya?"

"No, I guess I forgot to mention that. You want to spend some time working the knots out of me?"

Lisa, "Sure thing cowboy."

"I am no longer a cowboy. Now I'm a, a freight person, er whatever you call someone that does this kind o' work."

The barman, "That's a freighter."

Poe, "Oh thanks. Yeah, I'm a freighter."

Lisa, "Come on upstairs and I'll work the knots out of you real proper like."

Poe spent the night with Lisa and was loading his freight wagon the next morning when the sheriff came to the office to find him.

Sheriff, "You fixin' to go back to Timinsville again?"

Poe, "Why yes sir, Sheriff."

Sheriff, "Call me Farley. My name's Farley Higgins. Now I guess we know each other well enough to call one another by our first names."

Poe, "OK Farley, what's on your mind?"

Farley, "That fella that shot Ted was seen back in Timinsville since you left there, and the sheriff there sent me a wire to let you know that you might encounter him on the trail. So watch yerself, OK?"

Poe, "Sure thing. I'll keep my eyes peeled." With the wagon loaded and the team hitched up to leave, Poe said goodbye to Mr. Thompson, and was on his way back to the mining camp, via Timinsville.

Then he remembers the lovely Katie. A month ago he had no knowledge of women at all. Now he had two women in two separate towns looking forward to seeing him. All at once he wasn't sure if he was lucky, or not. Neither was a virgin, and he liked them both. Both worked in a saloon, and both were pretty. He would be a gentleman, and treat them both with equal curtesy and make a point of not getting too drunk and calling one of them by the others name.

He had driven several hours and could tell the horses were staring to tire a bit. So at the top of the next rise, he would give them a rest. The next rise was only about four hundred feet uphill, but it was a gradual rise and not too hard to make. A clump of trees near the top provided some shade from the sun looked like a good place to stop and rest the horses. Then he saw a rider move quickly in front of him, and then out of sight again. This could be trouble. Thinking this could be an ambush, he decided to rest the horses right there where he was, "Whoa!"

The horses stopped. He was certain that whoever was waiting for him, would be hidden in the clump of trees toward the top of this rise. He would wait him out. Instead of allowing the horses to rest in the shade for an hour to an hour an a half, he would instead let them rest for two hours in the sun.

Hopefully whoever was waiting to ambush him would have to wait as well, and with luck, he may become impatient and press the issue. He took some, water from the water barrel and gave each horse a healthy drink, and patted their necks and talked gently to them, to reassure them that he knew they were tired, and they could rest for a while. After forty minutes of waiting Baxter appeared in the road, and was headed in his direction.

Poe knew he could not out run him with a wagon load of goods, plus Baxter was in front of him. So he had to decide on what to do next. He checked the shotgun. It was loaded, both barrels. He also checked his six-gun. It had five shells loaded, better load one more. Then he waited, and waited, and waited some more. If he was going to survive an ambush, he had no other choice but to continue to be patient.

Finally, after an hour and fifty minutes, Baxter came out of the thicket with guns blazing. Poe got behind the wagon and waited for him to come into range of his shotgun. Two bullets passed by so close to him that he could feel the wind gush. Still not close enough, then BLAM, a bullet hit him in the shoulder, spinning him backward a step. He ducked down and felt another bullet rush past. *Now, he thought, don't miss.* When Baxter was nearly on top of him he raised up and fired, BOOM! BOOM! Poe dropped his shotgun and grabbed his pistol, and brought it up to his line of sight. No need. Baxter was lying in the road bleeding from the buckshot wounds all over his front side. Pistol in hand, he approached his assailant. "Damn you, kid you shot me!"

Poe, "You was fixin' to shoot me, so I don't feel the least bit sorry for you." Then Baxter collapsed, dead. Poe managed to tie him to his horse, behind the wagon, and continued on towards Timinsville.

Upon arriving, he stopped the wagon in front of the sheriff's office and got down. All at once people were slapping him on the back, and congratulating him on killing the man tied to his horse. "Good job son, that'll teach him to fool with you," and so on. Poe was trying to explain to all of these folks at once, that he was just trying to do his job, nothing more.

"Nonsense, you're a hero boy; that thar fella was a bad hombre, and we're all glad you got rid of him." Then there was Katie, throwing her arms around him and kissing him like he had been gone for years.

"Ouch gal," said Poe, "I got nicked a bit," indicating the small amount of blood on his shoulder.

Katie, "Oh I'm sorry darlin', I didn't know you was shot. We gotta get you to the doc's office."

Poe, "It's just a scratch; I ain't hurt none."

"You still need to go and see the doc and have him put some medicine on it and a bandage. You go on and see him right now, so it won't get no infection." After a brief visit to the town doctor, Poe went to the saloon to get a cold beer. Upon entering, everyone in the bar began to applaud.

The sheriff was also there and came up to Poe and handed him two hundred dollars. "Here you are Poe congratulations."

Poe, "I don't think I understand, what's this money for?"

"It's the bounty on that bad man you killed. It seems there was a two-hundred-dollar bounty on that fella for robbing a bank over in Mudville a couple of months back, only I didn't see the poster on him till after you left."

Poe, "You don't say. Since I'm rich today, drinks are on me." [everyone] "Yahoo, whoopee, yahoo."

"I'll be a one eyed rooster! I never would a thought I'd be so popular. I'm surely happy you folks are so glad to see me, but I still got to do my job. So I'll be leaving here for the mine, shortly."

"Oh no you don't, the miners were so happy that you shot that fella that they're sendin' someone to drive the wagon to the camp, and then back to here for you. So you just sit right down and enjoy yourself, and they'll take care of everything."

Poe, "I don't know what to say."

Sheriff, "Don't say nothin, just enjoy yerself."

Poe awoke the next morning with the second hangover of his life. Poe, "Oh my achin' head! Did someone hit me with a shovel er somethin'?"

Katie, "Oh no sugar; you just did a right good job of getting yerself so drunk you couldn't even make it up the stairs. Some of the men you bought drinks for, did that."

Poe, "Oh, I'll have to thank them for that."

Katie, "No need, they was happy to do it. And, your wagon's back and here's your money for the goods; it's all there."

Poe, "Again, I don't know what to say. Did we uh?"

Katie, "Me and your little friend had a real good time, you was sorta passed out, but that little friend o' yours was quite a trooper, and me and him finished up without you."

Poe, "You what!"

"Well darlin', I didn't want to waste the opportunity and he was surely willing."

"I'll have to have a talk with him. How about we go have some breakfast?"

Katie, "Sure thing sugar, I'll throw on some clothes and we'll do that very thing." At breakfast there were still people stopping by their table to thank Poe for killing an outlaw.

Poe, "Damn, I feel like I'm kinda on display here, and it feels kinda uncomfortable. I didn't do nothing all that special, I just did my job is all."

Katie, "Yeah sugar, but this is a small town where nothing happens, and when something does happen, then it's a big deal. Next time you come here, won't hardly anybody pay you any mind at all. That's just the way small town's is. You eat your breakfast and try not thinkin' on it too much." After breakfast, Poe went outside to see his wagon all hitched up and ready for the trip back to Ellensberg.

Appaloosa

Chapter 5

Poe was glad to be leaving Timinsville and getting back to Ellensberg, not only to escape the unsolicited attention, but also to see Lisa. He knew that sooner or later he would have to make a choice between her, and Katie, but not right now. Mr. Thomson said how glad he was to have hired such a nice young man, and didn't realize he had, in fact, hired a hero.

Poe, "I'm no hero, I was just doing my job. I wish folks would leave me be, I'm not used to this much attention. I would appreciate it if everyone would just forget about me, so I can feel normal again."

"It comes with the territory son. Folks out here in the west are starved for entertainment. So any time someone does something out of the ordinary they all of a sudden get a lot of notice. It's just the way folks are. Maybe if you was to take off to someplace for a week or so folks would forget you quicker."

Poe, "Don't you need me for the trips to Timinsville."

"Yes I do, but I figger you could make another trip tomorrow, and them miners would be set for a couple of weeks, and you could go and look around for that horse you're looking to buy, and speakin' of horses, you ever see a Appaloosa?"

"No sir, can't say I have."

"Well of all the horses the Indians had to choose from, they picked the Appaloosa as their favorite, on account of it's the most surefooted. It's not the fastest, not the most stamina, but the most surefooted, that is to say, the most reliable in a dangerous place, like a narrow pass through the mountains, and kinda tippy toe through them swampy places, and they ain't skittish either. Yep of all the horses in the West, the Appaloosa is the best. If you-uns can find one, that is. They're fairly rare. But, if you can latch onto one, you'll never be sorry for buying it. And, if you want to make the trip, I got a brother lives over yonder right on the boundary line between Kansas, and the Oklahoma territories, that buys and sells horses all the time, and if'n he don't have a Appaloosa, he'll know where to go to get one. His name's Bart, and if you want to go there, I'll send a wire and tell him you're a friend of mine, and you're on your way there."

Poe, "Gee Mr. Thompson, that'd be great, thank you."

"No problem boy; glad to do it. Now you go on and spend some time with that gal of yours, and I'll see you first light."

Poe spent the evening with Lisa and told her that when he returned from his next trip to Timinsville, that he would be leaving again to Oklahoma territory to see a man about a horse.

Lisa, "Oh I get it; you had your fun with me and now you're gonna leave me for some other gal. Who is she?"

Poe, "What?"

"That's just what men say when they're fixin' to leave a gal. I'm a going to see a man about a horse. There ain't no horse, is there?"

Poe, "Not yet, there ain't. I got to go there and buy it first, that is if he has a Appaloosa. Mr. Thomson said he was gonna send a wire and ask him."

Lisa, "You mean you really are going to see about a horse?"

Poe, "Yeah a course, there ain't no Appaloosas round here. None that I know of, and Mr. Thompson said that they were the best breed of horse there is."

Lisa, "Oh I'm sorry, I thought you was fixin' to get shed of me for another woman."

"I'm trying to get away from all these people a telling me I'm a hero, slapping me on the back, and making all this fuss, all on account

36

of me killin' someone. And, I don't care for it, so I'm going out of town for a spell, so they'll forget me, and I can feel normal again. I'll go soon as I get back from my trip to Timinsville tomorrow. I thought you and me could spend some time together before I go."

Lisa, "Who's the gal in Timinsville?"

"What? I ain't going to Timinsville, I'm going to the miners' camp, the other side of Timinsville, only it don't have no regler name, so I call it a trip to Timinsville. On account of I have to go through there to get to the miners' camp. You wanna go with me? There's plenty room in the wagon."

Lisa, "Four days in a dusty wagon, no thanks."

Whew thought Poe, if she had said yes he'd really have been in a fix. Then let's have another beer, and have a dance or two, and when I get back from the MINERS' CAMP, we'll talk about what we're gonna do after that, OK?"

Lisa, "Sure Poe. I shouldn't got so uppity 'bout where you were going in the first place, it ain't like were married er nothing."

The word married hit Poe like a thunder bolt. He hadn't even considered the possibility of marriage. He liked her sure enough, but he liked Katie as well, and hadn't considered marrying her either. "Lisa you know I like you, and all, but I don't know nothin' at all 'bout being married. Hell, my regular job keeps me away from town a few days at a time, I ain't got no house to live in, and I'm not sure I'd even make out at all as a husband. I'm only nineteen and this whole entire conversation's got me all twisted up inside. I'm gonna have me a whiskey and go to my room and turn in early, so I kin get a early start to the miners' camp tomorrow. I'll be seein' you when I get back, good night." Having said that, Poe kissed her and walked out.

He was up at dawn and was loading his wagon and thinking about the conversation with Lisa the night before, when Mr. Thompson came up to him and said, "Problems in paradise son?"

"Oh, morning Mr. Thompson; didn't see you."

"Poe we're friends. I think it'd be alright if you called me Bert, OK?"
"OK, Bert."

"Can I give you some advice boy?"

Poe, "Sure thing Mr., er Bert."

Bert, "Women are hard to figure out sometimes, so the best advice I can give you about them is, don't try to. They got different priorities then men folk. Women want security first, then they want kids, and then they want to please their man. But, they try to get the man first, figuring that once they have one they can work on getting the other two. Let me put it to you this way, if you had only one choice of what you NEED more than anything else, what would that one thing be?"

Poe, "A good horse."

Bert, "See? A woman would say a man. Then you'd probably say a six-shooter or a good rifle right?"

Poe, "Yeah, probably."

"A woman would say a house. Third you'd probably say a ranch er a farm, and a woman would choose kids. So you see men and women ain't that much different, they both want the same things, it's just that they want the same things in a different order of importance, is all."

Poe, "I think I'm beginnin' to see what you mean. Thanks a lot, Bert."

"You're welcome son. Now you can try and figure out which of them gals is best for you."

Poe, "You know about Katie?"

Bert, "You forget who made that trip before you did. Me, I just sorta filled in the blanks. You're a nice young fella and she's a pretty woman, it's a small town, and you're a fresh new face; wasn't too hard to figure out. Katie's a real nice gal, but I don't think she's even close to settling for any one man, right now. Plus, the fact that she don't ever run out of steam, you know she works two jobs, and don't sleep much, I'd bet that if she married a regular man, she'd wear him down to a nub, in no time at all. She's a very unusual woman in that regard."

"I think I understand what you mean, thanks Bert."

"You're welcome Poe, now you have a nice trip, you hear?"

Poe, "Sure thing Bert." The trip to Timinsville was uneventful, and he was now on the trail to the miners' camp. He usually only spent one night on the trail, and one night in town, but this trip he spent two nights out on the prairie, and on his way at sun up, and he only stopped long enough to water the horses and allow them to rest for an hour, before moving on to the camp. That way he wouldn't have to see or speak to Katie. Knowing in his heart that Bert was right about her, and she wasn't settling down anytime soon, and the less they saw each other the better for both of them. He would, of course, say goodbye to her when he returned from the camp. As usual, the miners had him unloaded and he was paid and on his way home in no time at all.

He pulled up outside the saloon and was on his way in to have a cold beer, and say goodbye to Katie, but was met at the door by the sheriff. "Hold up there Poe. I saw you coming and decided to head you off. You don't want to go in there right now, that fella you killed has two brothers and they're in there looking for you. If they don't see you they can't bushwhack you on the trail home, so do us both a favor and get on out of town."

Poe, "OK Sheriff, if that's the way you want it. I'll go, but you know I ain't afraid of them."

Sheriff, "Of course I do. Everybody knows you're not scared, I'm just trying to avoid trouble, if I can; that's my job."

"See ya, Sheriff."

"Bye Poe, and don't worry, I'll say goodbye to Katie for you."

Poe, "Thanks." Having been ushered out of town before his would be assassins could discover his presence, Poe only had one more piece of business; go and see Bert's brother and buy an Appaloosa, if he had one. With the pay from this last trip, plus what was left of the bounty money, and his room paid up for the next two months, Poe figured he could spend upwards of a hundred to a hundred and twenty dollars for a really good horse. And, barring any unforeseen accidents, like a severe injury to the animal, a horse was an investment, a good mount, a man could own and ride for years. "Bert, I'm fixin' to leave for that town, to see your brother. Oh by the way, what's the name of that town?"

Bert, "Oh yeah, Clarkston, Oklahoma territories, I wired him and told him to look for you, his name is Bart Thomson; he's my brother. Just look for somebody that looks like me. We're twins."

"You're joshin' me."

Bert, "No I ain't, sides Bart and me we got three sisters: Betty, Bertha, and Bobby Jo. Bart wired me back and said he had a Appaloosa, real good horse and you could buy it, but he'd want about a hundred and twenty dollars for it. But if you haggle with him, I'm sure you can get it cheaper than that. You see we're family and we don't see each other all that often, so if you don't tell him nothing about me and my job and what all's been going on here, then he'll come down on the price. That's 'cause he'll have a whole lot of questions 'bout me, so if you tell him, you ain't gonna tell him nothing, less he comes down on the price, then he'll sell it to you for less money."

Poe, "I think I understand."

Bert, "You just don't give him no information 'bout me, unless he comes down on the price of that horse. Don't worry he will. He'll probably invite you for dinner with my sisters and if you leave right now, you'll be there by supper time tomorrow."

"OK Bert, I'll leave right now, and thanks."

"You're welcome."

40

As Poe approached Bart's spread, Poe saw the horse in the corral, before he reached the ranch house. It was magnificent, fifteen hands high, and one fine looking animal. It was clearly the lead horse in the corral, as all the other horses gave way whenever it came near them. Yes sir, a horse like this would be well worth whatever he paid for it. But, he still recalled what Bert had told him.

"Hello in the house, anybody home?" hollered Poe.

"Howdy! You must be Poe; my brother told me to look for you. How is my brother anyway? Did he tell you about my other business?"

Poe, "Hold on Bart; your brother told me not to say nothing till we settle on a price for that horse."

"Damn his hide," said Bart, "I shoulda known he'd pull somethin' like this. OK, I want a hundred and twenty-five dollars for that horse, and I won't take a penny less."

Poe, "I guess I came all the way here for nothing. I thought we could do business, reckin' I was wrong." With that said, Poe turned his rental horse to leave, and Bart said "Now hold on young fella, we can still do some horse trading. How about a hundred an twenty dollars." Poe started to leave again.

Bart, "Wait, wait, wait how about a hundred an ten?"

Poe, "Is that horse been broke yet?"

Bart, "Sure he has, you want to ride him?"

Poe, "Of course, but only if I can buy him for say, a hundred dollars. Your brother don't pay me all that much."

Bart, "Oh, you work for Bert then?"

Poe, "Yeah, I'm his driver and loader."

Bart, "You're his driver and his loader?"

Poe, "Yeah, I was just loading, but his regular driver got hisself killed and I took over the drivin' part too."

Bart, "You don't say."

"It might be I could tell you all about it, for the sale of a hundred-dollar horse."

I tell you what, since you work for my brother, and I know how cheap he is, you tell me all about what's been going on there where he lives, and I'll sell you that horse for ninety dollars, and that's as low as I kin go."

Poe, "Sold, providing I can ride him. He looks to be a powerful animal."

Bart, "Here, give him this carrot. You give him this and he'll warm up to you faster."

Poe, with carrot in hand, approached the horse with his outstretched hand and talking in a smooth even tone of voice. "Here big fella, here's a nice juicy carrot for you. Easy now." Feeding the horse with his left hand, and rubbing his neck with his right hand while talking softly, the Appaloosa seemed to settle a bit. Bart gently placed the reins over its head, and then began to saddle the horse. Bart, "Did I say he was broke? Actually, he's only trail broke, but you show him who's boss, and if he gets to bucking too much, just spin him around in a couple of circles and he'll know to settle down."

Poe climbed up onto the animal and at once the animal reared up and then began to buck. Poe remembering what Bart had told him, took a firm hold on the reins and pulled it to the right. The horse turned to the right in a circle, and then another circle, and a third circle, and stopped. Poe turned him in another circle to the left twice, and stopped, and patted the horses neck, and then said, "Yah!" The horse took off like it had been shot out of a cannon. Running like a deer being chased by a wolf, this horse could really cover some ground. He gave the horse its head, and in no time horse and rider were one. A horse can tell a good rider from a novice one, and this animal could sense right away that Poe was an experienced equestrian, and responded to every subtle movement the man made.

Poe was thanking his lucky stars that he had spent all those months on the trial pushing cattle, as he had ridden several horses in the remuda, ridden in all sorts of weather and over every conceivable terrain. He slowed the horse to a walk, and turned back toward the ranch. This was one fine animal, and worth way more than a hundred and twenty-five dollars. He pulled up to the corral and dismounted, and again stroked the horses neck. *What will I call this magnificent beast? he wondered.* "Mr. Thompson, you got yourself a deal, now what do you want to know about your brother?" The men talked all through dinner, and half the night, on the subject of Bart's brother Bert, his job, the town, and anything else Bart could think of to ask about. Then Bart told Poe he was welcome to spend the night on his floor by the stove, but Poe insisted on sleeping in the stable with his new friend Ajax, the name he had given to his horse. The following morning, Poe was up and had Ajax saddled for the trip back to Ellensberg.

Bart, "I'll take back the rental horse for you as I got some business in town anyway. You tell my brother, I said howdy and be careful not to get hisself shot."

Poe, "Thank you for the horse, and I'll tell your brother everything we discussed, bye."

"Goodbye boy, you enjoy that horse."

Poe, "I'll surely do that, goodbye."

* * *

My Horse, My Friend

Chapter 6

Since he didn't have to be back at work for another ten or twelve days, Poe decided that he would spend some time with his new best friend, Ajax. He could feel the horse's strength beneath him, and although he had ridden several dozen horses when he was on the trail drive up from Texas, none of them had as easy a gait as this animal. Bart and his brother had been right about the sure footedness of an Appaloosa. This was far and away the finest animal he had ever ridden.

Once he was out on a flat area where it was safer to ride faster, he let Ajax have his head. "Yeah boy! let's go." With that, the horse took off like a shot, and once he reached top speed it was as tho' he was almost floating above him, instead of riding on him. Ajax was chewing up the ground at a tremendous rate of speed. After a couple of minutes of running flat out, he slowed the animal down to a canter, and then again to an easy trot, and finally to a walk. He knew for sure that what he was told about the Appaloosa was indeed true, and he could easily understand why the Indians would pick this breed of horse over all the rest. Barring any unforeseen accidents, Ajax and Poe would be together as man an horse, for a long time to come. He would make certain that this horse would have anything and everything a horse needed, regardless of cost.

After all, this was not only his basic mode of transportation, but a horse was company for a lone cowboy out on the range. He was also pretty darn sure that this particular horse was smarter than most. He surmised this when a gust of wind kicked up and blew off his hat, and before he could disembark, the horse grabbed his hat with its teeth and cranked its head around so Poe could take it from him. Yes, indeed this was some kind of horse, surefooted, fast, and smart, not to mention a very good looking animal. He was mostly white in color, with the grey mottled rear and a few spots here and there. Ajax had a coal black mane, and tail, with black hooves and was a very striking animal indeed.

Poe had only been in the saddle for ten or fifteen minutes, when a band of Kiowas let out several war cries and proceeded in his direction. It didn't matter the reason, the Indians had decided to attempt to run him to ground, Poe wasn't about to stop and ask why. As tho' on cue, Ajax took off like a shot, thundering across the plains as fast as he could go, and in no time at all had out distanced this obvious threat. Running as tho' on instinct, Ajax was way too much horse for any of the Kiowa ponies to keep up with him, and in a few minutes, Ajax and Poe were well away from them.

Although the Kiowa had tried to catch this Appaloosa, it got away. Tacheawana, the leader of the Kiowa band, had set his sights on this animal, and he would kill anyone to possess it. This was an Appaloosa and a horse for a chief like him, not some white man. He would track this man and his horse until he could capture them. Then after killing the man, the Appaloosa would be his. So he instructed the five braves with him to begin looking for signs of the man and his horse. Indians could tell one horse and rider from another by the imprint each one made in the earth. The horse had already proven that it was too fast to catch, but they could still track it down, and sooner or later they would be in a position to trap this elusive animal. It was just a matter of time. After all, the man had to sleep some time, and there was six of them, and they could all read signs. "I will have this horse said Tacheawana, it is a horse for a chief, not for a white man. With this great horse, I will become the greatest war chief ever. I will lead my brothers to victory over the whites, and drive them from our land forever."

After being chased by the Kiowas, Poe decided that the safest place for Ajax and him was in a Whiteman's town. Although the town of Shamrock, Kansas, was rather small in size compared to say Ellensberg, or his home town of Waycross, in Texas, he and Ajax would be infinitely safer here than alone on the prairie. So riding into town, the first place he would go would be the stable.

"Howdy stranger, you lookin to board your horse here?" said the stable man.

Poe, "Why yes I am, we were chased by some Kiowas and I don't figure to be out on the prairie any longer than need be. So I'd be ablieged if you could put him in a nice safe stall for a day or so. And, I want him to have a double ration of oats, he deserves it; he out run them Indians like they was standing still. I'll brush him down myself. We're still getting to know each other."

"Whatever you say mister." said the man.

"Oh, my name's Poe Dievers and this is Ajax."

"My name's Willis, and I can see why them Injuns was chasin' you. That's one fine animal, and a Appaloosa to boot. Injuns just love them horses and you wouldn't be the first man to lose a Appaloosa to them."

Poe, "I don't plan on loosin' him to Indians er no one else. You sure that this place is safe?"

Willis, "As safe as any other stable, I reckin'. I don't figger Injuns will come into a Whiteman's town to try and steal 'em."

Poe, "You got a hotel here?"

Willis, "Yeah, if'n you wanna call it that. It's the Starlight, right down the street on yer right."

Poe, "Thanks."

"You're welcome young fella." Willis could not have known how desperate Tacheawana was at obtaining Ajax. For that night after the Kiowas had tracked him to the town, he had instructed his band of warriors to steal Ajax from the stable in the wee hours of the morning, when the white men were all asleep. Willis usually slept in the stable with the horses, so he would always be available to anyone needing their mount in the middle of the night. So when Ajax smelled the Indians approaching he began to whinny loud enough for Willis to hear. Unfortunately for Willis, when he came to investigate, he was shot in the chest with an arrow. The three Indians that came to the stable to steal Ajax found that this horse was a lot more problem to handle than they thought. Ajax kicked the first Indian in the leg, and broke it, causing him to scream in pain. Then he began to buck violently as the other two tried to lead him out of the stable, all the while whinnying as loud as a horse could whinny. This woke some people up, and they came to investigate the noise. Upon reaching the stable and seeing Indians in the town, a cowboy shot and killed one of them running away from the scene. Poe was there too, reaching Ajax and trying to calm him down.

"Look," said someone; "they killed old man Willis, all because of that horse. You need to get that animal outta here mister."

Poe, "But we didn't do nothing to deserve this, we just came here to rest up a bit and we just got here."

"I'm sorry son, but that horse of yours is bad luck. Long as you're here them Injuns are gonna keep on trying to take him from you. Seeing as how they came into a Whiteman's town after him, means they want that animal pretty darn bad. It'd be easier for you to leave here than for the whole town to fight off a Injun attack. So you'll have to git."

"OK, said Poe we'll leave at first light. Right now I'm gonna sleep a couple more hours, so I can stay in the saddle, good night."

The Indian with the broken leg was hanged by the towns folk for killing Willis. Whether or not this was the Indian that had actually shot the arrow or not, didn't matter. The town had lost a stableman, and a friend, and someone had to pay. So the crippled Indian was elected.

With the deaths or two of the Kiowa band, Poe felt that the odds were changing in his favor. But now he was out on the prairie again, and he knew that this band of redskins was still out to steal his horse, and he would have to be ever watchful from here on. As darkness approached, Poe was elated to see a campfire in the distance. Seeing the size of the fire, this meant that it was indeed white men, and that was a good thing, because any white man would surely side with him when it came to Indians.

"Hey you in the camp, can I come in?" asked Poe as he

approached the camp.

"Come on in stranger." The camp was occupied by three men seated by the fire having coffee.

"Much ablieged. I was hoping to meet up with someone else out here. There's a band of Kiowas in the area and I didn't figure on spending the night alone out here, if I could help it."

"Come on in and have some coffee stranger, you can stake her horse out with ours over there."

Poe, "Thanks, my name's Poe Dievers, I just come from Shamrock. That's a little town east of here."

"Yeah, we was there a couple of nights ago. Ain't much of a town no how. My name's Wiley Simons, that guy's John Lester, and the other one's Jed Billups. Say, that's one fine looking horse you got mister; would you be looking to sell him?"

Poe, "Not on yer life, I just bought him a few days ago, and I plan on keeping him for a long time."

Tacheawana's most stealthy brave was Chemosh, and Tacheawana sent him on foot to creep up on the Whiteman's camp to determine how many there were. "There are only four, same as us."

"Then we kill them, and I will have the great horse," said Tacheawana, "come, we will go on foot from here." Creeping ever closer to the camp the Kiowas planned to ambush the Whiteman as they slept. But once again, Ajax smelled them and began to whinny loudly waking Poe and the others. Wiley stood up and yelled "Injuns!" and was shot in the back with an arrow, killing him instantly. All the men began to fire their six-guns at the attacking Kiowas. Killing two with their gunshots. Meanwhile, Tacheawana was untying Ajax and in no time at all was on him and riding away from the camp. John Lester was clubbed in the head with a tomahawk and died in a few minutes, but had shot and killed his attacker.

"Damn! they got my horse," said Poe, "I'll kill that Injun if I ever get the chance."

Ajax got up to full speed with the Indian aboard and after a mile or two when he felt the Indian's grip on the reins loosen a bit, lowered his head and stopped on a dime, throwing the Indian head first onto the sand. Ajax turned around and started back to the camp. Poe was saddling John's horse when Ajax appeared out of the darkness. "Well I'll be," said Jed, "I think that thar horse of your'n must love you for sure, looky there." Ajax went over to Poe to greet him.

Poe, "Boy, am I glad to see you big fella. You throw that Injun off did you?" Just as tho' the horse understood him nodded his head. Jed had taken an arrow to the shoulder and was in need of a doctor so the two men decided to go back to Shamrock as it was the closest town to where they were.

Upon seeing the man with the Appaloosa return, the town sheriff was on hand to meet them. What are you doing back here mister, we don't need no more Injun trouble.

Poe, "Hold on there, Sheriff. I just came back to get this man some doctoring is all. We got attacked out on the prairie, and he took an arrow, I just brought him here so's he could heal up. I'll go but I gotta tell you that there ain't but one of them Injuns left, and he's afoot. He tried to run off with my horse and Ajax throwed him off. So even if I was of a mind to come back here, he wouldn't be here for quite a spell, not walking here anyways."

Sheriff, "I guess you can stay for a day or so, but if we have any more Injun trouble, it'll be on account of you, so don't plan on staying here long."

"No problem Sheriff, I'll be gone day after tomorrow."

One on One

Chapter 7

Tacheawana was disgusted with himself for being thrown by the Appaloosa. He had been thrown off horses when he was a young brave, but never since he had become a chief. Once he had possession of this animal he would teach it to obey him, and since he was the only one left from the raiding party, no one else in the tribe would ever know, about his unceremonious ousting from the back of a horse. After all he was a chief, and as such was above other men in the tribe.

He knew better than to attempt to steal this horse from the Whiteman's town alone. So he would wait until he could take this man, out on the prairie, one on one. But for the time being, he was afoot, and alone. He remembered a farm house a few miles away where he could steal an animal to get him back to his tribe.

Poe told the sheriff that since the town's only stableman had been killed, because of his horse, that he would take over the man's job, until he left town the next day, and that he would spend the night in the stable with Ajax, to insure that Ajax and him would both be there the following morning. Sleeping fitfully, and getting up to check on his friend Ajax every few hours, Poe was not in the best of moods the following morning, and was more than happy to leave the town of Shamrock.

Where would he ride to next, he wondered, back home to Ellensberg, or to Timinsville, or perhaps just ride for a while and see some more of the country. After a little thought, he decided to head in a northerly direction, but also inclining to the west so he wouldn't be too far off track from the trail to Ellensberg. After several hours, he then decided to make camp and give Ajax a well-deserved rest. He now was quite certain that if anyone approached in the darkness, that Ajax would whinny loud enough to wake him. He would make a mental note to buy some carrots for him at the next town he came to.

The next town he saw was not more than a few buildings, housing about a hundred or so people. When Poe rode in, the first person that he saw was a young girl, and asked if she knew of anyplace he could buy some carrots. The girl's name was Sarah and she said that her parents had a farm nearby, and yes they had lots of carrots, and if she could ride on his horse home to the farm, she would show him where it was. "Sure thing young'un, here," reaching down for the girl's arm and pulling her up on to the horse, they proceeded out of town. Poe, "How come you were in town by yourself?" asked Poe.

"My ma sent me to town to find my pa, and tell him to come on home, but he didn't want to."

Poe, "Oh I see." Upon reaching the girl's farm, Poe could see Sarah's mother struggling to split a large chunk of firewood, with an ax. She had swung the ax hard enough to embed it in the stump, and now was struggling to free it.

Poe, "Here now ma'am, let me help you with that," Poe said as he dismounted. "This isn't no kind of work for a woman." With that, he pulled the ax from the stump and then chopped it in two, and then chopped the two pieces into two more pieces, and then split a few more, to make an armload of firewood. "There ma'am that oughta make a good fire. You need some kindlin'?"

"Well, I maybe could use a little," said Sarah's mother, "but you don't need to do it. I just had a might bit a trouble with that one big piece."

Poe, "Oh, there ain't much to it," said Poe, "I think the main problem is your ax is dull. If you got a stone, I could sharpen it for you." Before she could say no Poe took the ax an began to look around for a suitable stone to hone the edge. "This man wants some carrots ma," said Sarah.

"Oh, I'm sorry ma'am, my name's Poe Dievers, and yes I'd like to buy some carrots for my horse."

"Mister, you can have all the carrots your horse can eat, seein' as you helped me with the firewood, an all."

"Oh no ma'am, I'll gladly pay for 'em. I tell you what. I'll go on and split this pile of wood for the exercise, and then I'll pay you for the carrots. I just wouldn't feel right allowing a lady to do a man's work."

"My name's Alice Pickins. You met my daughter Sarah, and I got a son Beau around here somewhere. How 'bout I make a fresh pot of coffee for you."

Poe, "Thank you ma'am, that'd be fine." Poe was sharpening the ax and noticing that the farm in general was pretty run down, but with a little work could be a nice productive place. What a shame Sarah's father was a drunk.

He had only been working a short time when Alice's son came from around the corner, and asked, "What's that man doing here ma?"

"That man's name is Poe and he's here to buy some carrots, for his horse." Beau was a boy of fourteen and looked to be able enough to do a day's work, but apparently wasn't required to do so.

"Hey now mister, you-uns shouldn't be on our farm at all, you go on and git now, else my pa will shoot you when he gets home."

Alice, "You hush up that kind a talk, Beau. That man's been a doing your job, and you should be thanking him for it. So you just hush up that kinda talk and bring that kindlin' inside so's I can start a fire and make some coffee. Yer pa couldn't shoot nobody no ways; we ain't got no amintion fer that ol' shotgun, and he'll be too drunk when he gets home to even hold on to a shotgun. And, you're supposed to be feedin' the pigs anyway; did you even bother to do that?"

Beau, "Not yet, I ain't."

Alice, "Then go on and do it, and leave that man be." After thirty minutes of sharpening and then chopping up a dozen small logs, Alice called Poe into the house for a cup of coffee. "Here you are Mr. Poe, we even got a little sugar left, would you care for some?"

"Yes ma'am, just a little touch is enough, thank you." Poe had only drunk half a cup of his coffee when Sarah's father came through the door drunk as usual. "Who's horse is that outside, and who is this," seeing Poe through blurry eyes?

"My name's Poe Dievers and I brought your daughter home, and was looking to buy some carrots for my horse."

"Carrots my ass, you was lookin to have yer way with my wife, wasn't you?"

Poe, "What! You're crazy mister. Look, I don't want no trouble, I'll just be on my way." Poe got to his feet and pulled back out of the way of a punch aimed at him by the drunk man, that missed his target and the man fell over onto the floor.

"Harold, you drunken sot," hollered Alice, "you best be going on outside, if that's the way you're gonna act around compny, and this here man's compny. I fixed him that there coffee fer helpin' out with the firewood, somethin you shoulda done afore you left here. Now git on outside, if'n you're gonna act like this." Having said that, she helped her husband to his feet and pushed him out the door where he stumbled off the porch and into the yard. "This man just came here to buy some carrots fer his horse, and he was nice enough to help me with the firewood, since you wasn't here, like usual. Now you go on out to the barn and sleep it off, and take your worthless son with you. Here Sarah, take this here sack, go to the garden and fill it up with carrots, for Mr. Dievers' horse. Now then Mr. Dievers would you please sit down and finish yer coffee? Please!"

Poe, "Er a OK ma'am, if you think it's alright."

Alice, "A course it is; I said so, and since I'm the only one around here that works at all, at least for today, I'm the boss, and I'd like to thank you for your help and apologize for my husband."

Poe, "No need ma'am." Sarah returned with the sack of carrots and handed it to Poe, and asked can I feed one to your horse?"

Poe, "Sure Sarah, but just give him one. I don't want to spoil him."

Sarah, "What's his name?"

"Ajax," said Poe.

"He's surely one fine looking animal Mr. Dievers," said Alice.

"Thank you, ma'am. I just bought him a week ago, and he's already saved my hide from some Kiowas."

"Is they Injuns round here?" asked Alice.

"Oh no ma'am, that was a ways back down the trail, I figure they already went back where they come from." Poe could not have been more wrong, as Tacheawana had returned to his tribe and got another four braves to accompany him on another few raids and to look for the Appaloosa. They were watching Poe and the little farm from the ridge a quarter mile away.

"There's the horse, and the man. I will kill," pointing towards the farm. "Come, we will kill the Whiteman, and I will have the horse." With that, they all took off towards the little farm, and began to holler their war cries.

"Indians," said Poe. "Alice, take Sarah into the house, and stay away from the windows! Boy, take my horse to the barn, and tell your pa there's some shotgun shells in my saddle bags, and to shoot at them Indians from the barn. Go!" Poe grabbed his rifle and quickly loaded it to capacity, and then took cover behind one of the six by six inch vertical posts that held up the porch, and began shooting at the attackers. POW! One down four to go. The Indians rode around the house towards the barn and BLAM! BLAM!

Harold fired the shotgun killing another Indian, as they rode between the house and barn. Then, as they rode around the house again, Poe took aim and shot a third Indian, and Harold with two more blasts from the shotgun killed the fourth.

Tacheawana was now the only one left, and he rode out of range of Poe's rifle and sat facing the house, with his spear in hand, and was motioning for Poe to come out and fight him.

Alice, "What do you think he wants?" asked Alice.

"My horse," said Poe. "He's challenging me to a duel of some kind, him and me for my horse. This isn't the first time he's tried to take him, but it's gonna be the last time that he's gonna try."

Alice, "You ain't gonna fight him by your self are you?"

"Yes ma'am, I am. I'll die before I let him even touch my horse again." With that, Poe came out onto the porch, and yelled like an Indian, "Yee a hoo he! Beau, bring my horse!" The boy brought Ajax, and Poe climbed up and readied himself for the Indian's attack.

Tacheawana came straight at him hollering like a madman and throwing his war lance and just missing Poe by inches. Poe raised his rifle and began firing, BAM BAM BAM BAM. It took several bullets to hit his attacker on a galloping horse, but when he was done firing the Kiowa war chief lay dead, on the ground, along with the rest of his band. "I figure that's the last time I'm ever gonna worry 'bout him. Good riddance to him er anybody else tries to steal my horse. Thank you for the carrots ma'am. I reckin' I'll be going now, goodbye."

Wolves

Chapter 8

Poe left the carrot farm, and rode north for several miles replaying the incident of his fight with the Indian in his head. Two things were sure, Indians loved Appaloosas, and Ajax was one remarkable horse. On a whim, Poe decided to ride up to the mountains and explore the woods, and get away from people and towns and the civilized world, for a spell.

This, he told himself, would be good for his soul, and make the bond between Ajax and him even stronger than it was already. Man and horse together in the woods, they would go up to a higher elevation and be at one with the rest of nature, just Ajax, him and nature. After a few hours of casual riding, Poe got down to relieve himself, and Ajax took that as a cue for him to do the same. *Ahh, this is the life, a man and horse peeing together in the woods.*

After they had finished Poe got back up onto Ajax and they traveled on up the trail towards the summit. Upon reaching the top, he reined Ajax to a stop, and just gazed at God's handiwork. The forests, the mountains, the big blue sky with its puffy white clouds, all in unison painting a portrait like no one man could ever paint. It was truly a work of art, and breath taking to behold.

"Would you look at that?" exclaimed Poe, pointing at the horizon to Ajax. "Ain't that somethin?" Ajax exhaled through his lips as if to agree. "I tell you what; we'll make camp right here and be here in the morning when the sun comes up." Taking off the saddle and tying Ajax loosely to a clump of brush, so he could feed on the fresh grass around him. Poe then unrolled his blanket on a patch of grass and using his saddle for a pillow, lay on his back looking up at a sky that seemed to go on forever. *A beautiful night, a close friend, and good weather, boy you got it pretty darn good, he told himself,* and dropped off to sleep.

It was pitch black when the sound of Ajax's stomping and whinnying woke him during the early hours before dawn. He had just enough time to grab his rifle when the first of five wolves appeared in the campsite. The wolves attacked so quickly that he didn't have time to even bring his rifle up to shoulder level, before the first of the wolves was on him. Stopping the wolf's charge by catching the animal in the jaws with his rifle, and rolling over with him so Poe was on top of the wolf. Poe forced the metal barrel hard into the animal's mouth, breaking its jaw with a hard downward thrust, just as another wolf grabbed him by the leg and sank its teeth into his flesh.

Gritting his teeth and smashing the rifle butt into the animal's head, it backed off and charged again, and Poe squeezed the trigger with a half aimed shot BLAM! The wolf fell dead, but was immediately replaced by another one, which proceeded to jump on Poe, and this time the wolf got Poe's arm instead of the rifle. Rolling over and over with this animal and finally getting to his feet, he drew his pistol with his right hand and shot the beast twice, BAM! BAM! Then he quickly shot another wolf attacking Ajax, BAM! It fell dead and the two remaining wolves ran off. One of them limping badly from a vicious kick it had received from Ajax.

Bleeding from both his injured arm, and leg, Poe summoned his strength to toss the saddle up onto Ajax's back, and then collapsed from the effort. He knew he was going to need a doctor, but he first had to get to one. He managed to cinch up the saddle and throw his bedroll and saddle bags onto the animal before he collapsed again. He got up and put his rifle in its boot and as he put his foot in the stirrup, he talked to Ajax to calm him down. "Easy boy, easy big fella you just hold still for another second or two, and we'll get the hell out of this picturesque nightmare." Now he was headed down the mountain, but wasn't at all sure in which direction to go to find a doctor. Then he didn't have to, as he passed out from the blood loss.

Poe awoke to the smell of coffee, and felt a wet cloth wiping his brow, and when he opened his eyes, saw Alice. He started to raise up when Alice said, "Whoa now cowboy, you just stay right where you're at."

58

Then he heard little Sarah say, "Is Mr. Poe gonna die mama?"

Alice, "Not if we take care of him, Sarah."

Poe, "How did I get here?" asked Poe. "Yur horse brung you here last night. We weren't sure if'n you was gonna make it or not, it was touch and go for a while there. But once your fever broke this mornin', and the fact that you're young, probably saved you. What in the world happened to you anyway?"

"Wolves," said Poe. Where's Ajax?"

Alice, "Don't you worry none, he's in the barn, I told Beau to feed him good and brush him down, he looks to be fine no bites on him, er nothing. You on the other hand are likely to be here for a spell. So don't plan on getting out of that bed anytime soon."

Poe, "But isn't this your bed? I mean you and your husband's?"

"I ain't got no husband, he got hisself killed in a fight over in that saloon he used to go to. An I heard tell, it was over another woman, so don't you be a worrying yerself 'bout him. He weren't no good to us anymore, no how. Oh, he was a right fine man an a pretty good farmer for about fifteen years, but it seemed like a year or so after Sarah was born he just decided to be a drunk. He quit workin' the farm and didn't seem to care too much for the kids, er me, all he wanted to do was go to that saloon and drink till he couldn't see straight. He's been a doing that for a while now, so his gettin' killed weren't that much of a shock as you might think. I kinda figured it 'd happen sooner or later. I look at it this way; he was good while he lasted. Tryin' to scratch out a living here on the prairie is hard on folks, and my husband weren't the first man that this country broke. What with the blizzards in the winter, and the months without no rain in the summer, not to mention the occasional tornados, and windstorms, it's a wonder anyone can survive out here at all."

Poe, "I got some money, and I insist on paying you for all your help."

"You want to help, you get healed up, that's your job for now. When was your friends, er yer boss er whatever spect you back anyway?"

Poe, "Not for another week or so, I spect."

Alice, "Good, then you'll be our guest till you get healed up again. Now you lay back down there and rest. That's an order, I'm fixin' up some broth for you, and I want you to drink every bit of it, you hear?"

"Yes ma'am."

Alice, "And, would you please stop calling me ma'am. It ain't like we just met. You call me Alice, and I'll call you Poe, OK?"

"OK Alice." Alice and Sarah tended Poe for the next few days until he was able to get up and move around a bit. "I don't know what to do to thank you for all your kindness."

Alice, "I know one thing you can do for me, but you're not strong enough yet, so don't you worry yourself 'bout that right now. You want to go outside and sit in the sun, for a while?" asked Alice.

"Why yes ma, er Alice I think I'd like that very much."

Alice, "I tell you what, if you're all that set on helpin' out around here, you can split a little kindlin' with the hatchet. You sit here in this chair, and Sarah can fetch them little bitty logs over there for you, and you can sit right here and split 'em, and if you fill up the kindlin' box that'll be enough work for today, OK?"

Poe, "Sure thing, I'll have er done in no time a tall. But first I want to see Ajax." Poe started to rise when Alice gently put her hand on his shoulder and pushed him back down on the chair.

Alice, "You don't need to be walking to the barn. I'll have Beau bring him to you. BEAU! Bring Mr. Dievers horse around to the porch." Two minutes later Beau appeared with Ajax. Poe got up and stroked his neck, "Hiya big fella?" Ajax nodded his head and nuzzled Poe's hand.

Alice, "That horse surely knows who he belongs to."

Poe, "Yeah, he's probably the only friend I got."

Alice, "You mean you don't have no pretty young gal waitin for you somewhere?" Then Poe remembered Lisa. "I know a couple of gals back home in Ellensberg, er that is to say, I got a one gal in Ellensberg, that I sorta know, and a gal in Timinsville I talk to when I'm there on business."

Alice, "A uh, I figured you had a gal friend somewhere, a handsome young fella like you, but two gals, I'll bet you miss 'em both don't you?"

Poe, "Now, I ain't married er nothing like that!"

Alice, "I wasn't lookin to embarrass you none, and I didn't figger you was a virgin, are you?"

Poe, "Er a, well no ma'am, I mean—"

Alice stops him, "Tut, tut, now don't you go and break open them stiches; I think I know what you're trying to say, after all, I was a pretty young gal once."

Poe, "You're not old, and I think you're a right fine looking woman."

Alice, "You're a good liar, but thanks just the same."

"Oh no ma'am, I ain't lyin'. I know more than a couple of men a might older than me that would be tickled pink to have a woman like you, and that's a pure fact."

"Well thank you, Poe. That's right nice to hear, I haven't had no one tell me anything like that for quite a while."

Poe, "Well they should."

Alice, "Where are you from anyways? Timinsville, did you say?"

"Oh no, Timinsville is where I make my deliveries, for my job. I been living in Ellensberg, that's about sixty er seventy miles west of here, I think."

Alice, "Oh, I got some chores to do, so you work on splittin' some of that kindlin', and I'll get to doing them. Sarah you help Mr. Dievers with the kindlin'."

Sarah, "Yes mama."

Poe took a piece of wood and began to split slivers from it an inch or so wide, and put them into the box, and after only a few minutes began to perspire and tire a bit. "Whew!" he said to Sarah, "I didn't think that doing a little ol' job like this would tire me out so much."

Sarah, "Mama said for me to watch you and make you stop working if'n you got tuckered out at all."

"I'll be aright young'un, I just need to slow er down a might, is all." Although he was splitting the chunks with his right hand, his left arm began to throb where the wolf had bitten him.

"MAMA! Mr. Poe's getting sick again."

Poe, "Now Sarah, I ain't sick, I'm just a might sore is all, and a little bit of work ain't gonna hurt me none. Bring me another piece, please."

Just then Alice came around the corner of the house and said, "That's about enough for one day, Mr. Dievers. You need to go inside and lay back down."

Poe, "Just let me finish this last piece." With that he split the chunk in two and then grabbed it and split it again, and put the pieces in the wood box. "There said Poe, I don't figure that's enough work to even pay for my meals but I'll get stronger, you'll see."

Alice, "I'm sure you will, but no more today."

After another week, Poe was well enough to ride Ajax and had split a chord of wood.

After supper Poe went out on the porch to watch the sun set. Alice came out and sat down next to him, and looked at him as tho' he was the first man she had ever seen. "Poe, do you remember what you said awhile back about if ever I needed something, I should ask?"

Poe, "Yes Alice, and I meant it. What can I do for you, I owe you my life?"

Alice took hold of his hand and gently squeezed it and said, "Please sleep with me."

Poe's eyes widened, then before he could answer she leaned forward and kissed him ever so gently on the lips, and said, "My husband hadn't touched me for over a year, and then he was drunk. I'm still a woman, and I need a man sometimes just like a man needs a woman sometimes. I know I'm too old to marry up with, but could you please make love to me, at least for tonight. I know you'll be going back home soon, but before you go let me feel like a woman again, at least for tonight."

Poe didn't say anything after that, instead took Alice by the hand and led her to the bedroom, and the two of them fell onto the bed passionately kissing one another and exploring each other's bodies. Alice was only thirty-four and she had a lot of energy when it came to sex. She became a veritable wildcat in bed.

Once he was aroused, she took over, first writhing and thrusting her hips into his with the eagerness of a thirsty person too long without water, grunting and trying to exact every ounce of him. Her kisses were tender, and many, her breasts were full and firm to the touch, she had obviously held herself back a little at first but now she was grinding on him like this was the last time she would ever do this and sought to have every bit of him she could get. She bit her lip, so as not to awaken her children, as she churned and pumped, she ran her hands over his young frame. Finishing twice, he had fallen off to sleep, and three times she had awakened him with her desire for more.

Poe awakened at what must have been late morning or early afternoon, to the sound of Alice singing in the kitchen. Before he was even dressed, Alice was there with a hot cup of coffee.

Alice, "Mornin handsome, you wanta another ride?" Before he

could answer, she said "I'm just joshin', but I gotta tell you somethin' mister, if I was ten er fifteen years younger, I'd never let you go."

Poe, "Don't you go saying nothin 'bout your age now. You're woman enough for any two men, and I mean that in a nice way."

"Thank you Poe. I feel better'n I have in quite a spell, and you need to be getting' back to your job, else you won't have one. But now that I'm alone way out here, I might just decide to sell this place and move to somewhere where there's more people like Ellensberg."

Poe, "If you do, you be sure to look me up, and I'll do everything I can to help you get settled."

Alice, "You promise?"

"Yes ma'am, I promise." Then as the children were outside playing Poe leaned over and kissed her one last time. "I'll never forget you Alice."

Alice, "And, it'll be quite a spell afore I ferget you Poe. Goodbye now."

"Goodbye." Poe mounted Ajax and rode off toward home.

Homeward Bound

Chapter 9

In a strange sort of way Poe hated to leave Alice and her children, but knew that overall, it was for the best, and he hoped that one day he would see them again. For now, alone on the prairie with Ajax, and knowing he was headed home was all that occupied his thinking. *He had survived two Indian attacks, and a vicious encounter with a pack of wolves, which left him with some nasty looking scars, but, had gained the world's best horse. Was Ajax worth all that trouble? Answer, hell yes he was, not only was he the best horse a man could ride, but he was an excellent early warning system. Had it not been for Ajax's warning, the wolf scenario could have turned out quite different indeed. The Indians only tried to steal him because he's worth stealing, Poe continued to think to himself, you lucky son of a gun, you only paid ninety dollars for a three-hundred-dollar horse. In fact, as smart as he is, he might even be worth four or even five hundred. I'm going to take Lisa for a ride, when I get back. And you, my noble steed, no my friend, you are going to get a well-deserved rest in your very own stall, all the oats, and hay you want, and however many carrots is left when we get home.*

"Damn if that word doesn't sound good, HOME, he said it again, Home, we're going HOME! HOME! HOME! Come on boy, let's GO HOME, YE HAW!" Ajax took off at a gallop and was running like a freight train. But in Ajax's mind, home was back at the ranch in Oklahoma where Poe had bought him, and took the fork in the road heading that way. "Whoa, Ajax," said Poe. Ajax stopped and when Poe tried to turn him toward Ellensberg, Ajax seemed to resist the whole idea. "OK, I'm sorry I should have realized that what you think of as home is back there on the ranch in Oklahoma. NOT HOME, you got that, not home, we're going to Ellensberg, that way," pointing so the horse would know. Poe had never heard of a horse being so smart that a person would have to explain things to it. But apparently, that was the case. Not that anyone would ever believe him, should he be foolish enough to tell anyone. "This way boy, WE'RE GOING TO MY HOME, that way!" Once he had backtracked to the fork in the road, and got Ajax pointed in the right direction, he was on his way again. *Then it occurred to Poe that he had been with three different women and was only twenty years old, but as far as he knew, Ajax didn't even have a lady horse friend, so he would have to remedy that situation as soon as possible. You know if you had a female Appaloosa, you could start a horse ranch, and after a few years with Ajax as stud you could have one of the best strings of horses in the West, he told himself. Yes sir Poe Dievers, that's a right sound idea. But first he'd have to get back to work and start saving some money, as he had given some to Alice, and had not worked for a while now. So he would need to start making some money again as soon as possible.*

Upon entering town, he first went to see Bert Thompson, to explain his absence.

Bert, "Well, look what the cat dragged in. Is that the horse my brother sold you? Say, he's one fine looking animal, ain't he?"

Poe noticing that someone new was loading the freight wagon. Poe, "Who's that guy, and why's he doing my job?"

Bert, "He's not doing your job. He's doing his job. I had to hire somebody when you didn't get back here. Life goes on, and business is business. Sides that, I'm glad you're back so's you can do the driving again. I'm the one that's been going to Timinsville twice a week, and I'm getting too damn old to be doing that anymore. So I for one, am glad you're back. Let's go have a drink, and you can tell me all about your little vacation."

Poe, "Vacation, it was more like a nightmare. I've been getting attacked by everything, since I bought that horse."

Bert, "Where 'd you get that scar on your arm?"

Poe, "Oh, that was from the wolf that bit me, right after the two Indian attacks."

Bert, "Two?"

Poe, "Yes two, both times it was on account of they wanted my horse. The wolves I figure, were just hungry. Thank God for Alice er I woulda never made it back here at all. She's the lady that took care of me after the wolf attack. She's a widow now 'cause her husband got shot right after the second Indian attack."

Bert, "Sounds like you didn't get all that much rest while you was gone."

"Maybe so, but I got the world's best horse, I named him Ajax, and I got to go and put him in a stall, and feed him, on account of I promised him."

Bert, "You what?"

"I promised him, and a promise is a promise." With that said, Poe took Ajax to the livery and asked if Ajax could have a permanent stall there just for him. "Well I suppose that'd be OK, so long as you can pay in advance."

Poe, "How much?"

"Well let's see now, fifty cents a day, times thirty days is fifteen dollars."

"Here's five. I'll be right back." Walking back to the freight office Poe found Bert to ask for a small loan, to pay for Ajax's rent for the month.

Bert, "You know of course, that I don't generally loan out money, but for you I'll make an exception, for two reasons. First off, I was the one that sent you to my brother to buy that horse, and without him you wouldn't had so much trouble, and second, I figure you're a good risk. You can work it off a little at a time. The freight business has kinda grown since you were here last."

Poe, "Well, that's a good thing, isn't it?"

"Yeah, if I or rather we can manage to keep up with all the new business. I'm getting too long in the tooth to be working twelve to fourteen hours a day. If you hadn't come back for another week or so you might have lost your job. So, I'm real glad you're back. That new fella's name is Felix Hardgrave er somethin like that."

Poe, "Not Hargrove is it?"

"Yeah, that's it, Hargrove."

Poe, "Uh oh, it can't be. I think we may have a problem, Bert."

Bert, "How so?"

"That guy that I shot and got the bounty money for had two brothers, and guess what his last name was—Hargrove."

Bert, "You mean he's the brother of the outlaw that you killed?"

Poe, "Might be, maybe that's the reason he's here to kill me for shooting his brother. That don't sound like a good thing, now does it?"

"No it don't, but how we gonna know for sure?

Poe, "Well, I could get myself killed, but I don't think I'd like that very much."

Bert, "No, and I'd have to hire two more people if he did, and I don't want to lose you."

"Thanks, I appreciate that, now what are we gonna do to find out for sure if he's the brother of the other one or not?"

Bert, "It might be we can get him to show his hand. I figure that the only reason he hired on is to get a line on you, and if we set a trap for him, then we'll know for sure. Since I wasn't sure exactly when you'd be back here, I told him to come to work first thing in the morning to load the outgoing wagon for Timinsville. So if Hargrove goes to the telegraph office to send a wire to his brother to let him know you're coming. Then we'll know if he's who we think he is. Ol' Ned at the telegraph office an me been friends for years, and he'll tell me where he sent a wire to, if I ask him. So you don't say or do nothin to make him suspicious, and we'll just wait an see, if he sends a wire or not. I'll tell him to go to lunch and then we'll watch the telegraph office to see if he goes there. I'll tell him that you're going to drive the wagon to Timinsville tomorrow morning."

Poe, "Sounds like a plan, but what if he don't send no wire?"

Bert, "Then I reckin', we'll just have to think up something else. Why don't you go and say hi to Lisa, and you can watch the office from the saloon, if he goes in there. I'll tell him he's gotta load the outgoing wagon for tomorrow today, so you can leave at first light. Then when he's busy loading the wagon, I can go and see Ned."

Upon entering the saloon, Lisa saw Poe and ran over and hugged him. "Ow, easy gal."

Lisa, "You're hurt."

Poe, "No, "Just still a little sore from some trouble I had while I was gone."

Lisa, "Well, you shouldn't been gone for so long."

Poe, "Sorry, it couldn't be helped."

Lisa, "Let's get a table over in the corner, so we can talk a spell."

Poe, "No, I have to be here to watch the telegraph office."

Lisa, "Why do you have to watch the telegraph office?"

Poe, "I'll tell you later, just know that's it's important, OK?

Lisa, "If you say it's important, it must be. Can I at least have a welcome back smooch?"

Poe, "Sure." With that, he put his arms around her and gave her a firm, but tender, kiss, and then went back to watching the office. And, sure enough, after a half an hour, Felix was there and walked in. Five minutes later he left to return to work.

"Damn, I was kinda hopin' I was wrong."

Lisa, "Wrong 'bout what sugar."

"I'll tell you later. I gotta go now." Upon returning to the freight office, Bert saw him. Poe just nodded a yes." With that, Bert took a minute to introduce the man. "Felix, this is Poe Dievers, my driver. Poe that's Felix something er other. I'm sorry I can't remember your last name."

Felix, "It's Hargrove."

"Well, now we're all acquainted, Felix as soon as you're done loadin', you can leave. I won't need you no more today. Poe can you watch the office for me for a spell? I got to go and see my friend down the street 'bout our checker game this evening."

Poe, "Sure Bert, be glad to." Bert left to go to see Ned and confirm the wire message, and Poe was alone with Felix, the brother of the outlaw that he had killed. He couldn't let on that he knew what was up with Bert's new employee, and felt very uneasy just being that close to him. *Stay calm he told himself, just act natural, and pray that Bert returns soon.* After a few minutes Bert returned and nodded a yes to Poe. That meant that they had been right about the wire to Felix's brother, and Poe would probably be ambushed on the trail to Timinsville, before, or on the way back.

He wished he could just shoot this one, and then he would only have one to deal with later. But there was always the chance that this brother maybe wasn't wanted by the law, and if he killed him, he would be the one in trouble with the law. He guessed he would just have to play the hand out and see. Felix had just finished loading the wagon when Bert returned, and Felix walked up and announced that he had just received a wire message from home that his mother was ailing, and he would have to leave his job there in Ellensberg, and return to be with her.

"I understand. I'm sorry to hear that boy. You go on and go; here's your pay."

"Thanks for the work, Mr. Thompson," said Felix and left.

"Well Poe, I guess you were right 'bout him. He'll likely be waiting for us on our way to Timinsville."

Poe, "Us?"

"That's what I said us, I'm going too. I don't figure you can drive the team and watch for outlaws, and shoot said outlaws by yourself."

Poe, "Why? I done it before."

Bert, "Yes, but then there was only one of them now there's two, and I figure they're planning to rob me, after they kill you. So, I have a vested interest in going along on this trip; sides, I kinda got a hankering to see Katie again."

"You and Katie?"

Bert, "And why not, I knew her afore you did. Just 'cause there's a little snow on the roof, don't mean there ain't a fire in the furnace."
Poe, "A what?"

Bert, "I ain't too old is what I mean. Now you go on and get yerself a good night's sleep you're gonna need it. We got freight to deliver, and bad men to shoot tomorrow, and I want you alert. Now git."

Poe went back to the saloon to visit again with Lisa, and to say good night to her. He was glad that he didn't have to say anything to Katie when he saw her next.

* * *

Bushwhack

Chapter 10

Dawn was breaking when Poe awakened from a good night's rest, and he felt better than he had in a while, as most of his wounds were nearly all healed. He also felt hungry, and wondered if the cafe was open for breakfast. He would check to see if Bert was at the freight office yet, if not, he would grab a quick meal before the trip to Timinsville. Not seeing Bert's horse tied up out front meant that he probably had plenty of time for a bite to eat, and scribbled a quick note to Bert.

It read, "Bert having breakfast at café, join me. Poe". Seeing the cafe open, he walked in to smell bacon cooking, and the smell of fresh biscuits as well. *Mmm, he thought, bacon, eggs, taters, and biscuits, perfect.* He ordered some, and began to sip at his coffee, and told his stomach to expect something really good.

He was halfway through with his delicious repast, when Bert came in and said, "Good morning."

"Good morning to you too. You gonna have some breakfast, Bert? It's mighty tasty."

Bert, "I think I'll have a quick bowl of oatmeal, and some coffee. I had a pretty big dinner." The two men sat and ate for the next few minutes without speaking and then Bert said, "Poe, you know of course, that this might get a bit dicey out on the trail, seein' as how them yahoos are out to gun us down, don't you?"

Poe, "Yeah, I was just thinkin on that, and it seems to me that if I was to bring my horse with me, and sort of scout ahead of the wagon, that we might have a better chance to handle any trouble we might run into."

Bert, "You know boy, that's a right fine idea. Seein' trouble afore it gets there is always better than bein' surprised by it. You go on, and get that animal of yours and you can catch up to me on the trail."

Poe, "You got it, see you in a bit. Then he said to the waitress, "You tell that cook that was as fine a breakfast, as I've ever had."

Waitress, "Thank you, I'll surely tell him, as he don't get that many compliments fer his cooking. He'll appreciate that." Poe walked out of the restaurant and across the street to the stable. As soon as Ajax smelled him, the horse whinnied a hello. Poe walked up to him stroked his mane and neck, an then fed him the last two carrots, that were limp by now, but Ajax accepted them anyway, and munched them down. "You been in here restin' for a couple of days, you want to take a ride?" Ajax as tho' he understood, shook his head and pawed at the dirt nervously. Saddled and riding out of town, with a full belly, Poe thought for a minute of how well his luck had gone for the past few weeks.

He could have been much worse off, if things had gone differently. He had come a long ways from the boy he was when he had first come to Ellensberg with the trail drive. He had a good job, a girl friend, and the world's best horse. He was pretty lucky indeed. He nudged Ajax to pick up the pace to catch up to the wagon.

Ajax started to take off at a gallop, but Poe restrained him from running full out. "Whoa boy, we're not in a hurry," and slowed him to an easy canter. Pulling up alongside Bert, he asked, "Bert, what do you think of a man starting a horse ranch in these parts? You think that's a sound idea?"

Bert, "You mean with him?" indicating Ajax.

Poe, "Yes, I figure that if I could raise a few horses like him, I could sell them for a heap of money."

Bert, "I spect you could at that. He's a real fine animal. But you're talking years of breeding, and you're gonna need a ranch first, don't you think?"

Poe, "Well, I know that. I just wanted your opinion, is all."

Bert, "I might even go in with you on it, if you don't mind too much. I could get a loan on my business for a ranch."

Poe, "I don't want you getting yourself in debt 'cause of me."

"Look Poe, I don't have no kids of my own, and I think you're a right fine young man, and I'm always looking for sound investments. What you just described is as sound as any I've heard in a while. I tell you what, since my brother's found you that horse, maybe he can find another one."

"A mare," said Poe, "so Ajax can be a father, or at least have a mare to come home to, like a man has a wife to come home to."

Bert, "I never heard of anyone putting it that way before, but maybe you're right. Most folks figure that a horse is just a dumb animal, but me, I think just like you do, that horses have feelings just like people do, and if'n that's so, then having a mare to come home to makes sense to me." The two men talked as they rode along the dusty trek to Timinsville, with Ajax tied to the rear of the wagon, until they reached the halfway point, where the road began to rise in elevation.

"Bert, stop the wagon." Bert reined the team to a stop. Pointing to the rise, Poe said, "Up there near them bushes is where that hombre was going to ambush me the first time, and it's my bet that his brother's will try for us there also. It's the best ambush spot around because you can't see if anyone's there until it's too late. They're not expecting a lone rider, and they've never seen Ajax before, so I'll ride on up there and see if it's clear, you wait here. I'll be right back."

Nudging Ajax to a trot, Poe was past the clump of brush without incident, and signaled to Bert to come on. With most of the trail being flat both men were fairly certain that any ambush they might encounter would be on the way back home. They were right as the Hargrove brothers had decided to kill Poe, and anyone with him on the way back to Ellensberg, and rob them as well. After all, what did they need with a wagon load of goods, they didn't have the time or the inclination to sell them. But if they killed the men on the return trip, then they would have the money from the sale of the goods.

That was the way that Baxter had described it to his brother Felix.

"That's 'cause I got the brains in the family, and you got the muscle. That's why you was the one got the job a loadin' wagons and not me."

Pulling up to the front of the saloon in Timinsville, Poe and Bert got out and stretched, and then went inside to see Katie and some of the regulars they had talked with in the past.

"Howdy Bert, you old outlaw, how ya been? Hey Poe, you're back. Welcome boys; have a beer with me," said an old farmer that each had talked with in the past. Then Katie came up and kissed Bert on the lips, and then turned to Poe and did likewise, and said, "Hiya fellas, let's all have a beer. Now if you two don't mind me sittin' between you, then one of you has to move over a stool."

Poe said, "Yes ma'am, glad to." Katie sat down and said, "I didn't expect both of you to show up here at the same time, but I'm glad you did, 'cause you two are my favorite out of town customers. I for one, am glad to see you both." With that said, she raised her glass in a toast, "Here's to out of town customers with manners."

"Here, here," said the men.

Bert, "You know kid, if we only have one, we can hit the trail and be up at that camp and back by dark, if we hurry."

Poe, "Sounds good to me. Let's do that," and downed his beer. After having unloaded all the freight from the wagon, Poe was about to whip the mules into action when Bert said, "Hold on a second, we need a little something from them. You boys care to sell me back a couple a three sticks of that dynamite?"

"No, but you got a need for some, take all you want. You boys expecting some trouble, are ye?"

Bert, "Let's just say it's better to have some and not need it, than to need some and not have it."

"You're dang sure right about that partner," said one of the miners.

76

With the wagon unloaded, and empty the ride back to Timinsville was a breeze, and both were sitting at the bar when Sheriff Winters entered. "Howdy Poe, ain't seen you in a spell. You come along this trip for protection from bandits or are you just lonesome for our town?"

Bert, "I brought him so if those yahoos are gonna try to kill my favorite employee, I wanna be there."

Winters, "You are expecting trouble then?"

Bert, "Yeah, one of them brothers came to work for me while Poe was away, only I didn't know who he was."

Sheriff, "No wonder I haven't seen him in a while."

Bert, "Yeah, he quit just in time to beat us here, and tell his brother we were coming, but I got a nice surprise for them, if they try anything. And, since we didn't see them on the way here, I'm sure we'll run into them on the way back."

Sheriff, "I wouldn't be surprised, that older one, Baxter, he's usually the one does most the talking, probably all the planning too. Now the fastest with a six-shooter was Bob, and Poe there already shot him, so it's just the muscle and brains left, and they don't have all that much of either. So don't you two worry that much 'bout them. Oh, and I'm pretty sure that you're right about them ambushing you on the ride back, on account of I already searched the whole town for 'em, and they ain't nowhere to be found."

"Thanks for that, Sheriff."

"No problem, just doin' my job."

Bert to Poe, "Well, let's get to it. We gotta face them sooner or later; may as well get it over with. We do er just like we did coming up, you scout, I'll drive."

Poe. "You got it." The men left and rode all day without incident, made a night camp, and were back on their way the following morning. A few hours had passed when, BAM BAM BAM, bullets were coming from both sides of the trail. Two shots from the right and third shot from the left. Then another shot, BAM. Bert picked up a stick of dynamite and tossed it as far as he could in the general direction of the bullets. A few seconds later, KABOOM! The dynamite exploded. There was a short scream, and then silence. Felix was dead, blown apart by the blast. Then two more shots from the right and another stick of dynamite was thrown in that direction and KABOOM! This Baxter brother however, was smart enough to run in the opposite direction away from the blast. Unfortunately, he ran right into Poe sitting on Ajax, right in front of him.

Poe, "Don't try it." Baxter reached for his pistol, but was too late on the draw and Poe fired and killed him. Poe, "I told you not to try it." Poe came riding into view. "We got 'em," he said.

Bert, "Yeah, I reckin'. It's too bad they couldn't just give up; I hate to kill anybody."

Poe, "It was their call, they didn't give us no say in the matter, and we'll split any bounty money for them. Let's load 'em in the wagon." Once loaded, Poe asked, "Do we turn them in back in Timinsville, or take 'em back to Ellensberg?"

Bert, "I'll tell you, I never like to run over the same ground twice, if I don't have to. So, since we're already half of the way back, let's just wait till we get back to Ellensberg to turn them in to the law." Then he turned to the corpses and asked, "You fellas comfortable back there? Good, no complaints. Let's go home." As soon as the two men pulled up to the sheriff's office, the whole town turned out to see the bodies of the outlaws. Sheriff Higgins came out and said, "Hi ya boys, who's these fellas?"

Bert, "Howdy Farley, this here is Bad Bob's brothers. Is there a bounty on these two?"

Farley, "Matter of fact, there is, two hundred dollars apiece. You shoot both of 'em?"

Bert, "Nope, Poe got 'em both, so you can give him the bounty on them."

78

Poe, "Oh no, we're partners fifty, fifty."

"OK, but I'm using my half to buy a Appaloosa mare. Poe and me are gonna start a horse ranch."

Farley, "Is that so?"

Bert, "Yes sir, I'm going to send a wire to my brother to find us a mare Appaloosa. Let's go to the saloon and celebrate, first rounds on me."

A Lone Kid From Texas   T. J. Rowdy

* * *

A Visit from Alice

Chapter 11

It had been two weeks since Poe had left from the farm, and even tho' it had only been one night of love making, one night was all it took for Alice to feel like a woman again, and wish for the company of a man. Her husband Harold had not been much of a help around the farm, for a few months, and now that he was dead and gone, she wondered why she was even still there. If Indians attacked again, or bandits, or just a couple of bad men, looking for easy prey, she and her family would be hard pressed to stop them. Beau was fifteen now but a long ways from being a man, and probably wouldn't be much help, if they were beset by outlaws or Indians. So in her mind, the best thing she could do to better her circumstances, would be to sell the farm and move elsewhere.

"Beau hitch up the wagon, I'm going to town." Once in town, she went to see Mr. Bortles, the owner of the bank, and the man to talk to about selling her farm. After an hour about land prices, the rising cost of doing business, and just exactly how much her farm was actually worth, Mr. Bortles said, "I'd love to give you what you asked for, Mrs. Pickens, but the market ain't what it used to be when you folks moved here. There just isn't as much money to be had for a farm around here, like before."

Alice haggled with Mr. Bortles for as long as she could, and the two finally arrived at a price they both could agree on. With the money in hand, she would go back to the farm one last time, load up the kids, some of the furniture, and whatever else she could think of to bring, and leave for a new place. A bigger place with more people, and more of pretty much everything that the little town of Shamrock didn't have. *Alice thought to herself, now where did that nice young man say he came from? It was west of here, only what was the name of that town? Ellensberg, that's it!*

"Children we're moving to Ellensberg, Kansas. Anything you want to keep, you better make sure it gets in the wagon, 'cause we ain't coming back here." Alice and her children were on the trail to Ellensberg for three hot, dry, dusty days, and Alice only had to beat Beau once. Now that he was all of fifteen years old Beau had decided that since his father was no longer in charge that he was the man to make decisions for the good of the family.

"Oh, is that so?" said Alice, "You got a heap of growing up to do before you're in charge of anything young man, and if you think for one minute that you're man enough to make decisions for Sarah and me, you'd better think again."

Beau, "Pa's dead, and that makes me the boss of the family. So you ain't gonna whup on me no more, now you get in the wagon and I'll drive the team."

"You'll drive the team? Oh no you won't, and don't you go thinkin' you're a man yet, 'cause you ain't." Alice grabbed the reins from his hands and whipped him profusely with them, as he retreated around the other side of the horses to get out of range. He climbed in the back of the wagon and remained silent for the rest of the day.

On the evening of day three, they arrived at Ellensberg. *This is more like it Alice thought. It was easily three to four times the size of Shamrock, with a dress store, a restaurant, and a really nice looking church at the end of town.* "Here we are kids, Ellensberg, Kansas. Now let's all look for a bank to put our money in."

"Is that a bank, mama?"

Looking where she was pointing, "Yes sweetheart, that indeed is a bank. As fate would have it, Bert was just coming out of the bank just as Alice was coming in, and the two met in the doorway.

"Oh, pardon me ma'am," as Bert stepped aside for Alice to enter.

"Thank you sir," said Alice, "it's nice to know that there are some gentlemen here. I'm Alice Pickins. My family and I just now moved here from Shamrock, that's a little bitty ol' town a ways east of here."

"Oh, I'm Bert Thompson. I run the freight office down the street, and may I say welcome to Ellensberg, and if there's anything you have a need for just call on me."

"Why thank you, Mr. Thompson."

Bert, "Please call me Bert, and may I say that it's refreshing to see such a pretty gal as yourself picking our quaint little town to move to. I'm sure you and your husband will be very happy here."

Alice, "My husband's dead, he got hisself killed awhile back."

Bert, "Oh, I'm sorry to hear that, you got children?"

Alice, "Yes, I have a son fifteen and a daughter seven. Can you tell me where I might find a hotel for the night?"

Bert, "Sure thing ma'am. It's right down the street on your right; you can't miss it."

Alice, "Thank you again, Bert."

"You're quite welcome ma-er, Alice." Bert watched Alice as she climbed up onto the wagon, and silently kicked himself for not helping her up. She was a fine looking woman, and wondered if he should ask her to dinner tonight or wait till later on. While he was deciding, she drove away, down the street. *Now where did say she was from? Oh yes, Shamrock. That name's sounds familiar; where have I heard that name before? Oh well, perhaps it'll come to me later.*

Bert went home still thinking about Alice and decided he would call on her the following day. The next morning Poe was busy loading the wagon for a short run to Diggertown, a little spot in the road about eighteen miles away. "Good morning Poe; say you ever hear of a town named Shamrock?"

Poe, "Yeah, that's the town I told you about where those Kiowas came to try and steal my horse, and then that lady and her kids helped me after the wolf attack."

Bert, "Her name wouldn't be Alice, by any chance would it?"

Poe, "Yes, that's the lady that took care of me, who lost her husband. Why?"

Bert, "You better put that box down so's you won't drop it."

Poe loaded the box and asked, "Why?"

Bert, "That lady and her kids are here in Ellensberg."

Poe, "No!"

Bert, "Yep, that's a fact. I met her yesterday at the bank. Seems she sold her farm, and moved here, and I think I'm gonna ask her to dinner, she a right fine lady."

Poe, "You don't say. You sure she said her name's Alice?"

Bert, "Yeah, I'm sure, about so tall [indicating her height by holding his hand up], and pretty blond hair, and says she's got two young'uns, a boy and a girl."

Poe, "Sounds like the same woman, I wonder why she moved to here?"

"Maybe she's looking for you?"

"Yeah, now Bert, I liked her fine but, I ain't ready for no readymade family er nothin like that. We only had that one—"then he stopped his conversation.

Bert, "One what, boy."

"Well Bert, you may as well know, I slept with her that one night, on account of she nursed me back to health and she begged me too. But I didn't know she was gonna come here an—"

Bert, "Just hold on now. I'm not mad er nothing. I know you wouldn't do nothing unkind or deceitful, it ain't in you. I just wanted to know if it was the same woman er not; appears she is. So don't be too surprised when you see her. I figure to ask her to supper one of these evenings."

Poe, "You mean you and her, er gonna—"

Bert, "Gonna have supper maybe, and if we get along, who knows. You go on and finish loading the wagon and we'll talk about it when you get back from Diggertown, OK?"

Poe, "Sure Bert." Upon returning from his deliveries, Poe saw Alice and her kids sitting with Bert in the restaurant, looking like a regular family. He was glad that they had met, and twice as glad that Bert was not the least bit jealous of his liaison with Alice. He had told Bert of the brief affair but knew he was smart enough not to feel indifferent about it. He would run into her sooner or later so he might as well go inside and say hello to them.

Much to his surprise little Sarah stopped eating and came running to him as soon as she saw him. "Poe!" said Sarah and kissed him on the cheek as he lifted her up and hugged her. "Hiya stranger," said Alice, "long time no see."

Poe, "Hello Alice, I see you met my boss."

Alice, "Yes I have, but you didn't tell me he was so handsome."

"Now Alice, that ain't so," said Bert.

"Tis so," said Alice, "now I know two men in town, and they're both right fine fellas." Together they said, "Thank you,"

Alice, "Poe you want something to eat?"

Poe, "Oh no, I'm going to the saloon to get a beer. Nice to see you again, ma'am."

"Bye Mr. Poe," said Sarah.

"Goodbye Sarah. See you in the mornin' Bert."

"Good night, Poe."

A Lone Kid From Texas   T. J. Rowdy

* * *

Convict Outlaws

Chapter 12

Ben Morisey, and Clyde Hendricks had just been released from prison after serving five years for armed robbery, and hadn't eaten in two days. They were out on the prairie, walking, and desperately searching for anything they could find to better their circumstances, namely a horse, preferably two horses, two six-guns, some food, and of course, money.

Clyde, "I tell ya, I can't keep a walking like this fer too much longer, my feet are killing me."

Ben, "You just hold on a bit longer, there's sure to be somebody come by, or we'll find a farmhouse er something out here. Sides, we ain't got no say in the matter. I for one, don't figger to ever get myself throwed in to prison again, ever. So as far as I'm concerned, anybody we come across, is fair game, and it don't matter none who they are, or where they come from, long as they got somethin' I need."

Two more hours of walking, and he saw what he had been hoping for, a farmhouse out in the middle of nowhere. "Looky there Clyde, a farmhouse, and from the looks of it, there can't be too many folks a livin' there, maybe only one or two."

Clyde, "You figger they'll feed us? I mean, if'n we ask 'em nice?"

"You can ask. I don't ask, I take. You go on up to the house and ask whoever comes to the door for some water, and tell 'em your horse broke his leg, out on the prairie, and that's the reason you-uns is walkin'. Then, I'll sneak around behind the house and come up on 'em afore they catch on there're two of us."

Clyde, "Then what?"

"Then, we kill 'em and get what we need."

Clyde, "You mean, just up an kill 'em fer no reason?"

Ben, "We got plenty a reason. We got a need for whatever they's got, that we can use. Now, go on an get their attention, and I'll do the rest." Ben Morisey was no stranger to killing, as he had already murdered a family of four, for a mere twenty dollars, before he was arrested for the hold up in Sandstone, Colorado, with Clyde Hendricks, his new partner in crime. By the time the bodies were found by a drifter, he was already in prison, so no charges had been filed.

Ben, "Let's wait till dark, then whoever's in that place, won't see me coming around the back. You just go on up there and tell 'em you're lost an hungry, and get their attention, and I'll do the rest."

"Anyone to home?" hollered Clyde, as he approached the farm house.

"That's far enough mister; what's yer business here?" asked the farmer.

"Water, I just need a drink of water, if'n it ain't no trouble. My horse broke his leg and I been a walking fer a spell. I'm Clyde Hendricks and I ain't looking to cause you no harm, I just need me some water, is all."

Chester Matelin had lived in his little shack for more years than he could count, and rarely if ever saw anyone else, so being suspicious of strangers was expected. Chester, "How come you don't have no pistol? If your horse broke his leg, then how did you put it down?"

"I didn't," said Clyde.

Chester, "You mean to say that your horse broke its leg, and you just left it there to suffer?"

Clyde, "Well, I didn't have no choice, I couldn't very well strangle it, could I?"

Chester, "I reckon not, only it's a sad thing to lame a horse and not put it out of its misery."

"Like you said—"Ben hitting him on the head with a large rock, Chester fell unconscious and the two men hauled him inside, tied him up, and began to rifle through the house for food. After eating everything they could find, and not finding any money, and only three shells for the farmer's shotgun. Ben said, "Shit, I thought he at least would have an old pistol we could take, so's we'd have some protection."

Clyde, "At least, he had a shotgun."

Ben, "But, only three shells. I figure that this old timer's got some money, er maybe some gold, hid out here somewhere. We'll ask him as soon as he wakes up."

Clyde, "What if'n he don't wake up?"

"Well then, dumbass, we can't ask him, can we? Go on out to the barn an see if'n he's at least got a horse, we kin ride." The old man awakened to see the two outlaws seated at his table, eating the last of his food.

"Two of you, I mighta knowed; a man can't trust nobody in these parts."

Ben, "Oh, you're awake, good. Now, you can tell us where you hid your gold, old timer."

Chester, "Gold, you damn fool; I ain't got no gold, never did, probably never will have. I live here by myself, just me and my mule, Daisy."

Ben, "Come on old man, I know you got some gold hid out here someplace, so you'd better tell us where it's at, or we'll have to hurt you some."

Chester, "You already bashed my head in, you don't figure that hurt?

Ben, "No, now, I'm gonna hurt you, if you don't tell us where your gold is hid."

Chester, "I already done told you, I ain't got no gold. I maybe got three dollars for grub, but that's all I have. Take it, and leave me be."

"Ok, old man, I reckin' we'll have to do it the hard way." Locating a kitchen knife Ben tested the edge—dull. "I guess I'll have to put a better edge on this, if I'm gonna do any real carving."

Chester, "Oh please mister, honest, I ain't got nothing. I ain't never had nothin'. I live out here alone with my mule, and I prospect a bit but I ain't never found nothing, I swear."

Ben, "Last chance old man, you better tell us where your gold's hid."

"I already done told you I ain't got no gold."

Ben, "Then I reckin' you're diein' fer nothin'." Then Ben began to slice the old man across the chest, hollering, "Tell me where it's at." The old man just screamed and insisted that he hadn't any.

Ben Morisey was for all practical purposes, a sadist, and actually enjoyed the suffering of others. It seemed that the more the old man screamed the more he enjoyed the event. Clyde on the other hand, became sickened by the torture and had to go outside and away from the house, so he could no longer hear the screams and desperate pleas from the old man, that was being sliced to death an inch at a time.

After the old man died, without telling Ben what he wanted to know, Ben said, "I guess he was telling the truth, and really didn't have any gold after all. Well, at least he's got a mule, so we won't have to walk no more. You got any idea how far the next town is?"

Hold Up

Chapter 13

There was no ambiguity about the intentions of Clinton Moss, Jess Mavory, and the Farmer brothers, Sidney and Cecil. All four had taken part in the last three robberies of a stagecoach, and two banks in the towns they left before coming to Ellensberg. All four were wanted by the law, all had posters on them, and none cared for anyone else's life, but his own. Ruthless, vicious, and downright cruel were the words of the dying sheriff of the last town they had hit.

Four wanted men, unafraid of lawmen, the law in general, or anyone looking to stop their onslaught of terror. Once they decided on a target, it was business as usual. Find an easy town to rob, one without any law, or only one lawman, and maybe a deputy. They'd kill him, rob the bank, and usually abscond with one or sometimes two women to abuse later, after they had left town with whatever they chose to take. But, they were careful too. As a rule, they probably would have left the town of Ellensberg alone, because of Sheriff Higgins and the overall size of the place, but since the last three robberies had gone off so well, they all, to a man, felt more brazen, unstoppable, and nearly invincible.

Still Clinton, the undisputed leader of the gang, always did a pre-robbery check first. He rode into Ellensberg first, posing as a roving gambler just looking for a game. Then after a few pertinent questions, about how many lawmen there were, and calculating the haul versus the risk, would meet up with his other compatriots for a final plan, and according to his information, this little town was ripe for plucking. After a couple of beers at the saloon, all the while engaging anyone he could find to talk with about the information he needed, he left to acquire a room at the local hotel, and waited for the others to arrive. Knock knock knock. Opening the door, he saw Jess Mavory, his unelected second in command. "Where's them other two yahoos?" said Clint.

Jess, "They'll be along in a few minutes, we didn't want to look too suspicious by all of us coming at the same time."

Clint, "Good, you're payin attention to details. I like that. Have a drink, and when they get here, I'll lay it out for you." Eight minutes later another knock at the door, and there stood the Farmer brothers.

"Come on in boys, I'm pretty sure I got us a right good plan. First off, I want you two, to go out of town a ways and find a farmhouse with a small family of three or four, shoot the ol' man and rape the woman and make sure one of them kids is loose so's he or she can run to town to fetch the sheriff, and then, when he's out of town, we can rob the bank or freight office er whatever else there is. Just make sure the farm you pick is a few minutes away from town, so by the time the sheriff gets back to town, we'll be gone. If we ain't gone, then I reckin' we'll have to kill him too, and a coarse anyone else that might get in the way."

"Why don't we just kill the sheriff first?" said Jess.

"Because, lawmen pay closer attention to what outlaws look like more than folks that are scared half to death do. So if he don't see us, then he won't be as sure of who it is, exactly. And, we're not the only outlaws in the country, so if he don't have a positive idea of who did the robbery, maybe he'll take off chasing some other gang. The only thing that would make it a perfect robbery, would be if it rained, then there wouldn't even be tracks to follow."

"Maybe we should wait till it rains," said Cecil.

"You see any clouds in the sky?" said Clint.

"Nope."

Clint, "Me neither, so we'll go as planned. Now I want you two to go far enough out of town to do your lawbreaking, so by the time the sheriff gets there, we'll be on our way out of town with the money, in the other direction."

"That's a right smart plan Clint," said Sidney.

"That's why I'm the boss. Now go and make sure it's some place that has a wagon or at least a horse, so that whoever goes to fetch the sheriff, can get back here in oh a half hour or so. Now go."

Linda Summers was hanging clothes on the line, and her husband Marty was plowing out in the field, and their children were playing nearby in the creek. The farm was a good ten to twelve miles from town, and it had taken the farmer brothers at least thirty minutes to get there. So anyone going for the sheriff, it would take at least ten to fifteen minutes of hard riding to get to town an at least that long to return, so this place was ideal.

Cecil to Sidney, "You go out there and shoot her husband, and I'll get to raping his wife, and I reckin' that boy's old enough to ride a horse into town, to tell the sheriff."

Sidney, "But, I want to rape her too."

Cecil" "You can, right after you shoot her husband, it won't take me long. Now go on."

Sidney rode out to the pasture to shoot Marty, while Cecil closed on the woman.

Cecil, "Howdy ma'am, can I water my horse?"

"Sure mister, help yourself."

"I believe I will," and walked up and ripped open her blouse and slapped her hard in the face. She screamed, and Marty stopped working and had just turned around in time to get shot by Sidney BAM! BAM! Marty fell to the ground.

Willy, hearing his mother scream and the two pistol shots, knew on instinct that his parents were being attacked, and told his younger sister to stay where she was, and he would go for help. Willy, seeing one man riding towards the house and hearing his mother screaming, from inside, knew there was at least two men, and ran to his father's side. [Weakly] "Boy, unhitch the horse, cough, cough, an go for th the sheriff, hu, hurry." Willy unhitched the horse and led it a couple of feet closer to the plow so he could use the plow for a step to get up onto it. Then he whipped it and hollered, "Yaw!" The old horse took off at a gallop towards town.

Meanwhile, Clint and Jess were sitting in chairs pretending to read the paper across from Sheriff Farley's office, while they waited for the news to hit town. The Farmer brothers rode in an tied their horses to the hitching post outside of the saloon. Figuring they had enough time for a quick shot of whiskey before the bank robbery.

Willy struggled to hang on to the horse's mane as it galloped toward town, the horse was pretty old to be ridden that hard, and began to lather up as it gave its all, and finally collapsed an died before they could get all the way into town. Willy took off running and was so out of breath when he reached Sheriff Farley's office he could barely speak. Panting and trying to talk he said, "Sheriff, they they shot shot my pa, and my my ma was sc scream in from from in the the house. Our old horse da died gettin' here."

Farley, "Sit down son and catch your breath, how many was there?"

Willy, "Ta two, was all I saw." Just like Clint had planned, the sheriff got on his horse and rode out of town at a gallop, toward the Summer's farm.

Clint, "That's our cue, let's go." The two men got up and walked over to the bank of Ellensberg and drew their pistols, walked in an announced, "THIS IS A ROBBERY. DON'T NOBODY DO NOTHIN' FOOLISH, and you may live through this. You there," pointing his six-gun at the teller, "put all the money in a bag and do it quick." Albert Cummings the bank teller did as he was told and within a minute both Cecil and Sid were there to ensure that no one would interfere. Clint grabbing up the money sack said, "Thank you for your generous donation to the outlaws' fund," and walked out the door.

All four men rode out of town in the opposite direction of the Summers farm. All rode hard, until they were well away from the scene of the crime.

Aftermath

Chapter 14

The four outlaws rode for several miles before they decided that there was no one following, and stopped for a short rest.

Clint, "Now, that was the way all our robberies should go. None of us gets shot, and we don't have to kill nobody, and we get away clean as a whistle. Yes, sir, it sure pays to plan things out ahead of time. Now we can divvy up the loot, as soon as I get it counted. First we'll separate the ones, and fives, from the tens and twenties, and the fifties, and hundreds, from the littler bills, then we make four equal piles. Cecil, you count the ones, and Sidney you count out the fives, and Jess you take the twenties, and I'll count the big ones, on account of I'm the boss."

Clint, "On second thought, the wind is picking up, let's put it all back in the bags, and we'll count it later when we get to a hideout with a table and no wind a blowin'. We don't want to lose none of our hard earned pay to a windstorm. Let's rest the horses and try to figure where we can go to find a nice cozy hideout. Any of you know of some place we can go, to lie low for a while? No, well we'll just ride awhile, till we do. I figure after going a half a mile up stream in that last stream we crossed, it'll take any posse following quite a spell to find the tracks where we came out again, so we should have some time. All of you keep your eyes peeled for a shack or an abandoned cabin."

Sheriff Farley was mad at himself for being duped so easily, by the bank robbers. "Damn my eyes, I shoulda figured that attacking that boy's family was just a ploy to get me out of the way, so they could rob us."

Bert, "Now Farley, you don't be blaming yourself, them outlaws are obviously not amateurs, they planned this to a tee, which means they're pretty smart; just be grateful that no one was killed."

"I am grateful for that, only if I don't catch these guys and return the money, this place will be a ghost town in about a month. Most of the folks that had money in that bank are just common folks and with their savings gone, well I just shoulda known better is all. Now how many of you can I count on for a posse to go after these fellas?"

"I'll go," said Bert.

"Me too," said Poe.

"I'll go with you Sheriff," said Melvin Stubs, a rancher.

Silas Burke, a farmer, said, "And me."

"I'll go," said Tom Givens."

Farley, "That's six, anybody else? Anybody know a good tracker?"

"I know of a Sioux Indian over in Pepperville that can track pretty good," said Silas.

"Will he track for us?" asked Farley.

"We can ride there an ask him, but we'll probably have to pay him something. Do you know him?"

Silas, "Sorta. I don't know whether or not he'll remember me, but I'll ride over an ask him."

"OK, you do that. The rest of us will try to pick up their trail outside town. If we get a trail to follow, you an your Indian friend can meet up with us, when you get back here with him. OK let's ride."

After searching for signs of newly formed tracks, the posse was on the trail tracking the outlaws, when Silas rode up with the Sioux Indian. Silas this here is Tucinnae. I explained our problem to him and he said he'd track 'em for a price."

Farley, "How much does he want?"

"He said a dollar a day and a guarantee of ten dollars, whether it takes two days er a week."

"That sounds fair enough," said Farley, "let's ride."

Tucinnae got down and studied the ground for a couple of minutes an announced that there were four men and the tracks were fresh enough to follow. The posse waited for a bit to allow the Indian to get out ahead of them and keep on the trail, and they followed behind. After a few hours, they came to the stream where the bandits went in, an did not come out the other side.

"OK everybody, it looks like they went either upstream or down so you fellas go down stream and the Indian and us will go up stream and anybody sees tracks comin' out, fire a shot, and the rest of us will come a riding."

Twenty minutes later Tucinnae fired a shot up stream, and the posse was on its way again. "This Indian really knows his business," said Farley. "He said their only three hours ahead of us. If we hurry, we can be close by dark." When the men made night camp the Indian said they had closed the distance to an hour, or an hour and a half. "Tomorrow, we find."

"OK men, the Indian says we'll likely be on those buzzards by tomorrow, so everybody get some sleep, we'll be leaving at first light."

Clinton hands Sidney a spyglass and says "Sid, I want you to go to the top of that rise [pointing to a summit] and watch our back trail. If you see someone following us come riding as fast as you can and tell us. Now go."

Sidney was looking through the spy glass but let the sun catch the glass and made just the slightest glint show. That was all the Indian needed to know where he was. Tucinnae rode back to tell Sheriff Farley.

"Man up on hill there," [pointing to where he had seen the glint from the spy glass].

"Can you catch him?" asked Farley.

"Tucinnae only track, no fight Whiteman."

Farley, "OK. OK Poe, you think you can sneak up on that fella, if the Indian can show you where he's at?"

Poe, "I'll try."

"Good, if you can catch him we'll meet you at the fork in the trail about five miles from here. Good luck."

Poe stayed close to Tucinnae as they ascended the rise hoping they had not been seen, by whoever was at the top. Nearing the top, Tucinnae put his finger to his lips to indicate to Poe they were very near and to get down from Ajax and travel the remainder of the way on foot.

Luckily, Sidney had not seen them and was completely unaware of their presence, until he heard Poe say, "Drop your pistol mister. You're covered." Sidney whirled around to shoot, but was not fast enough and Poe was forced to shoot him. BAM! The bullet hit Sid in the shoulder and he dropped his six-gun in the dirt.

Poe, "Now that wasn't too smart now was it?" Hearing the shot, all the outlaws knew that it must have been Sid, warning them. They quickly mounted their horses and began to ride away from the area.

"What about my brother?" said Cecil.

"He knew the risks," said Clinton, "he probably fell asleep er something, anyway we can't fret about him now, we got to get to that fork. I got an idea of how to slow them up." Reaching the fork in the road, he said, "Tie some brush on the back of your horse an fire it. We'll burn the trail behind us, and then, when we reach the fork, they won't know which way to go. Wait," checking the wind first, "looks like we're riding into the wind, that's perfect the fire will hit them straight on. That'll slow them down."

The fire on both sides of the road was intensifying as the posse approached the fork, and the smoke was smothering. So, in the interest of safety, Sheriff Farley called a halt to the pursuit. Then Poe and Tucinnae appeared with Sidney tied to his horse.

"Howdy, Mr. outlaw," said Farley, "where's your friends?"

Sidney, "You go to hell Sheriff. I ain't telling you nothin'."

"Is that a fact? If you want that bullet out of you, you 'd best be telling us all about your friends, and if you do, we'll send you back to town to see the doc. Now if you don't tell us, then we'll just have to take you with us and if you don't bleed to death, you'll likely get gangrene. You know what that is? Gangrene is the color your skin turns if you don't take the bullet out, and you get all swoll up like, and then you get real weak an sick, an the wound starts to stink from the rotten flesh an—"

"OK, OK, I'll talk, only you gotta promise to get me to a doctor."

"Deal. Now we already know, there was four of you, what I want to know is where are you fellas heading, and do you have any extra horses?"

"I don't know where he decided to head for, and no we just got the ones we're ridin on."

"One more question, who's in charge of your merry little band? What's his name?"

Sid, "Name's Clinton, Clinton Moss."

Farley, "You don't say. He's wanted in quite a few places, if my memory serves. Yes sir, a thousand dollars reward on him. Now then who wants to take him back to town?"

Melvin Stubs, a rancher, said, "I will, I need to get home and feed my stock anyway. Do I still get to share in the bounty money, Sheriff?"

"Sure Melvin, you're still part of the posse, when you get him locked up go get the doc to fix his arm so he'll be healthy enough to hang later."

"You got it Sheriff. See you back in town. We'll be there."

Clint to the others, "Good, that oughta hold them up for a spell. Let's ride." The three men took off at a gallop, and then slowed their horses, after a few minutes and surveilled their back trail. It appeared that the posse was still some ways behind them; now they had to lose them completely.

"Let's split up," said Clinton. "It's easier to shake two, then three to shake six, so everybody pick a direction. I'm heading west."

Cecil, "I was gonna head west."

Clinton, "Now you can't, unless you wanna fight about it?"

"Never mind, I'll head north."

"I reckin' I'll go South," said Jess, "only I ain't goin' no where's without my cut."

"Look Jess, we don't have time to split it up here. I'll give you your cut of the money as soon as we get shed of this posse."

"Then give me a hundred, so I can get a room, an stable my horse, and have some money fer grub."

"YEAH, me too Clint," said Cecil.

"OK, OK, here: twenty, forty, sixty, eighty a hundred, now ride. Sixty, eighty, a hundred, go. I 'll meet up with you in El Paso in a week, if you get there."

Jess, "Oh, I'll be there. You just make sure you're there with the money."

"Don't worry 'bout' me, I'll be there." An hour later, the posse came to the place where the three men split up.

"Yeah, I was afraid of this. They split up, and went in three different directions, Silas, take Tom and go west and if you lose them just go back to town. I'll take Bert with me and go south. Poe you stick with Tucinnae and go north. After you run yours to ground, come an find us. OK, let's go."

With Tucinnae tracking, Poe was on the outlaw within an hour. Seeing him just ahead and noticing his horse beginning to falter, Poe knew he all but had his man. Poe nudged Ajax from a trot to a gallop and in no time at all, he was close enough to throw a lasso around him, and pull him off his horse into the dirt. Uh umff! THUD! Cecil hit the ground hard, knocking the wind out of him. When he got his breath there was Poe sitting on Ajax holding a pistol on him. "Unbuckle your gun belt, real slow like," said Poe.

Cecil knew he was caught and complied. "Tucinnae, my friend, would you be a pal and tie this hombre to his horse for me, please?" After securing Cecil to his horse, they headed back to town.

Meanwhile, Clinton was lying in wait for Tom and Silas, with a rifle. As soon as the two men were well within range, he fired twice. Crack, Crack. The first bullet hit Silas in the chest and he died almost instantly, the second round hit its target as well, but only wounding Tom in the side, not killing him, but he was in bad shape, and could not continue the chase. Clinton thought, *Well, I got my two, and if the rest of them get caught, then it's more money for me.* He turned his horse south, towards Mexico.

Jess could see his pursuers from his vantage point on a hill overlooking the trail he had just ridden over. *It figgers. I'd get trailed by the sheriff, said Jess to himself. No matter, he'll die as easy as anyone else,* and loaded his Winchester to full capacity, and waited for his targets to get a little closer to ensure a perfect shot.

Sheriff Farley was no amateur when it came to tracking outlaws, and had been ambushed a time or two before, so he was ready for whatever treachery this outlaw may decide to employ. "Hold up a minute Bert. If you were this outlaw, and you wanted to ambush us where would you be right now?"

Bert, "If it were me, I'd be right up there," pointing to the outcrop of rocks.

Farley, "Yeah, that's just what I figured, too. What do you think you'd do if you were him and we just sorta stopped right here and made camp?"

Bert, "I guess I'd sneak down here and wait for us to bed down and sneak down here and shoot us."

Farley, "Yeah, that's what I figured, too. You carry an extra shirt in your saddle bags don't you, Bert?"

"Yeah, but why?"

"We're gonna make a couple of dummies to stand in for us, and we'll wait this guy out."

Bert, "Dummies?"

Farley, "Yes, if we stuff a bunch of grass in our extra shirts, and put our hats on them, from a distance, he'll think it's us."

Bert, "Oh, I get it; when he comes down to ambush us we'll ambush him. Good plan Farley."

"Yeah, if it works." The two men made a fire and two dummies sitting having coffee, complete with bedrolls, then they hid in the brush nearby. They didn't have to wait long, as no sooner had night fallen and they could hear their quarry creeping through the brush toward the make believe camp. A few minutes later, and BAM BAM BAM BAM BAM. Jess, "Hunt me, will you; take that Sheriff," and walked into the clearing.

Farley, "Drop your gun, you're covered," as he walked into the clearing with pistol in hand.

Jess knew if he tried to fire his last shot, that even if he could out shoot one man he would surely be killed by the other, and surrendered. "You're a sneaky som bitch, Sheriff!"

"Yeah, I guess so, but all's fair in love and war. You're under arrest for bank robbery, murder, and rape."

"I didn't kill no body, and I didn't rape no body neither. I only helped to rob the bank is all."

Farley, "You'll get your day in court, just like your friends when we catch them."

Jess, "You ain't gonna catch Clinton, he's too smart for ya."

Farley, "We'll see about that, now get on your horse, and don't do nothin' stupid 'cause I don't have any qualms about shooting you and burying you out here on the prairie, after what you did to that family."

"I didn't do nothin' to that family," said Jess.

"Like I told you before, you'll get your day in court."

Bert and Farley rode into Ellensberg with their prisoner, to see Poe and Tucinnae sitting in chairs by the jail.

Poe, "Congratulations Sheriff, I see you brought my boss back, and you got your outlaw. We got ours; he's inside all locked up safe an sound."

Farley, "What about the other one, and the money?"

Poe, "All this one had was a hundred dollars."

Farley, "This one too. I'll bet the money is with the leader." Later that evening, Tom rode into town, barely alive. He had tied himself to his saddle so he would make it back, as he knew that when you give a horse his head, he'll always come home to his own stall, and since his horse would have to go through town to his ranch, he would make it back.

A cowboy, getting some air outside the saloon, saw Tom as his horse walked by, and stopped him. "Sheriff Farley! Sheriff Farley, come quick."

Tom, "Silas is dead. Outlaw got away from u uus—"and passed out.

The old doctor removed the bullet from Tom, but was unable to keep him alive and he died in the night.

Farley, "Damn, now I got to tell his wife, I got her husband killed."

Bert, "You didn't get him killed."

Farley, "I'm the sheriff, and I'm the one that took him along, so I'm responsible."

"I don't envy you none, Farley," said Bert. "What about the other one and the town's money?"

"I'll have to go after him as soon as the trial's over."

Poe, "You wait till after the trial, and he'll likely be long gone to Mexico, and we'll never get the town's money back."

Farley, "I got no choice. I have to be here when the circuit judge comes, to testify at their trial."

Poe, "I'll go after him, if I can take the Indian to track for me."

"I'd appreciate that Poe, if you think you can handle it alone. I reckin' the town can afford to pay that Indian for tracking, but we'll have to ask him."

Poe, "I'll go ask him, we got along pretty well out in the trail, so maybe he'll go with me."

"You got the thanks of the whole town son. You bring that hombre back here for trial, and bring back the town's money, we'll all be in your debt for a long time."

Hunted

Chapter 15

Clinton had ridden nearly nonstop, until he was out of Kansas and into Oklahoma, Territory, heading for Texas, and eventually on to Mexico. Figuring that if the others didn't show up in El Paso after a week of waiting, that they had been captured. But true to his word, he would wait till the week was up before moving on. For now, it was a soft bed at the hotel, a pretty gal to spend time with, whiskey to drink, and no worries about the law. Maybe he would even get another gang together and hit a few more towns, before retiring in Mexico. Yes, the life of an outlaw is good.

Poe was already to leave to start his pursuit of the last outlaw with Tucinnae, when the idea hit him like a thunder bolt. *Take the train.* "Tucinnae my friend, I won't need you after all, I'm going to ride the iron horse."

Tucinnae, "Whiteman not need Tucinnae to track?"

Poe, "No, my friend I don't think I will, but thanks anyway."

"Whiteman sure of this?"

Poe, "I'm sure. Thanks, you can go on back to your people."

Tucinnae rode off and Poe, excited at his idea, rode back to see Sheriff Farley. Coming into the office, Farley looked surprised. "Poe, what are you doing back here? You didn't change your mind, did ya?"

Poe, "Nope, I got a better idea. All I need is a tiny piece of information, about where them fellas are going. If we can manage to make one of them talk, then I can take the train and get there before him."

Farley, "That's right, ain't no horse in the world can outrun a train. That's a right smart idea, Poe."

Poe, "I thought so. Now we just got to get one of them fellas to talk about where Clinton Moss plans to hold up and wait for 'em. Who do you think will be the easiest to break?"

Farley, "Oh, that's easy, the one with the bullet in him, what's his name?"

"Sidney, yes good ol' Sid."

Farley, "First, we need to separate them from each other. OK, Sid, come on out of there," Farley said, as he unlocked the cell door.

Sid, "Is the doc back yet, 'cause my shoulder's really startin' to hurt and I think I'm getting that grandgreen stuff."

Farley, "That's gangrene and now that you mention it, I got some good news, and I got some bad news. The good news is the doc's back in town, and as far as I know he's never lost a patient to GANGRENE. The bad news is if you don't tell me where your partner with the money is headin, I ain't sendin' for the doctor at all."

Sid, "YOU CAN'T DO THAT, SHERIFF! I'm a citizen, and I got a right to get this here bullet out of me. I can't go to no prison with a bullet in me."

"Then you better tell me where Clint's heading."

Sid, "I ain't gonna tell you nothin'."

Farley, "Suit yourself, and you're right, by law, I can't send you to prison, er no where's else with a bullet in you, and even if I wanted to not tell the doc you been shot, eventually I'd have to. But the law don't say nothing about WHEN. So you don't want to talk that's fine by me, you can go back to your cell and the longer you wait to tell me what I want to know, the longer you're gonna suffer. And, the longer you wait, the closer you are to gangrene in that shoulder. You know, I heard tell of a fella that had a gunshot just like yours, and he waited too long to get to a doctor, an the doc had to take his whole arm off. But, it's your arm so you enjoy it while it's still there, you know you look a little peeked you better get some rest, I'll tell the doc about your arm tomorrow, maybe the day after." Having said that, Sheriff Farley closed the cell door, and then the door to the back of the jail, with Sid screaming insults. "You dirty som bitch, I'll kill you fer this you low down sidewindin' yellow #@%&*"

Farley looks out the window and sees the ol' doctor heading for his office. "Poe, quick, doc's coming; head him off."

Poe, "Howdy doc, how are you today?"

"Fine Poe, and you?"

"Oh, I'm feeling kinda poorly doc. I think I need some pills er something. I got a powerful aching in my stomach, can we go to your office and you can give me something for it, if you're not in a hurry er nothin'."

Doc, "Well come on with me, and we'll get your stomach fixed up." Seeing the doctor do an about face towards his office, Sid started hollering even louder.

Doc, "What was that fella in the cell sayin' about a bullet in him?"

Poe, "Oh, that's one of them outlaws we brung in and he's kinda crazy, is all." An hour later with his arm swelling, and hurting, Sidney finally relented and told Sheriff Farley that Clint was to meet them in El Paso.

"Thanks Sidney, I'll tell the judge that you helped recover the town's money, maybe he 'll go easy on you and I'll go get the doc, now."

After purchasing a train ticket to El Paso, Poe decided to take Ajax along with him, to ensure he had a good mount in the event he had to follow Clint into Mexico. Talking to Ajax to try an calm the horse, Poe said, "Easy now big fella, we're just going on a little ride on the choo choo, you'll be alright." Poe also took the best picture of Clinton Moss available. Now, all he had to do was get there ahead of him and wait. Poe got there, took a room at the hotel, and was in the El Tortuga Verde Cantina [in English, The Green Turtle Saloon] having a cold beer, and coyly asking of the whereabouts of one Clinton Moss.

"I don't know no one by that name mister," said the barkeep. "What's he look like?" Poe knew better than to show the poster on him so he gave the barkeep a rough description from what he remembered from the circular.

Poe, "He's an old friend, but don't tell him I'm here, I want to surprise him, OK?"

"Sure mister," said the man. Poe hung around the cantina sipping at his second beer and trying to formulate a plan to capture the outlaw without endangering any innocent bystanders. *Maybe I should wait and take him out on the prairie, with no one else around, but what if I miss him leaving and he gets away and I have to go to Mexico to get him. Maybe he's faster on the draw then me? Maybe he's already got another gang together? These were the questions Poe would ask himself for the rest of the day. Well, I guess I'll get some sleep, maybe he'll show up tomorrow.*

The following morning, Poe was seated at a table in the town's only eatery, when he saw Clinton Moss, ride in, but not alone. With him, were no less than three of the roughest looking men he had ever seen. *Damn, now what am I going to do, he thought. I better send a wire to Sheriff Farley, and let him know what's up.* Poe walked over to the telegraph office and sent a wire to Farley. To Sheriff Farley at Ellensberg, Kansas, stop. Found Clinton, has three men with him, stop. May have to go Mexico, stop, signed Poe.

"Is that all mister?" asked the clerk.

"That'll do, thanks," said Poe. Poe decided that even with a shotgun and a well-placed ambush, that the chances of taking all four men in a gunfight was not a certainty. He would allow them to ride from town and try to find a way to apprehend them on the trail.

Clinton asked, in response to the barkeep's comment about someone looking for him, "What did this fella look like?"

Barkeep, "Oh, he was young mid-twenties. I'd say, dark hair blue eyes, medium build, about six feet tall, said he was a friend of yours."

Clint, "That's funny, 'cause I ain't got no friends. You see him in here?"

The barkeep looks around, "Nope, he ain't in here, maybe he left town."

Clint, "Yeah maybe, or maybe he's a lawman or a bounty hunter. You see him again, you tell me, you hear?"

Barkeep, "Yeah, sure thing, I'll tell ya. You fellas want something to drink?"

Clint, "Yeah, give me a bottle, and four glasses." The four men went to a corner table to drink and talk. Poe was faced with the fact that he probably should let the Sheriff of El Paso know all about one Clinton Moss, and that he had another gang of outlaws with him. Knock knock knock. "Come in," said the sheriff, "what can I do for you, stranger?"

"Howdy Sheriff, I'm Poe Dievers from Ellensberg, Kansas, and I'm here looking to catch me an outlaw name of Clinton Moss."

"The Clinton Moss?" asked the sheriff.

Poe, "The very same, and he's here in your town, and he's likely here to either to rob your bank, or kill someone, or both."

"And, you know this, how?"

"I know, because he robbed the bank in Ellensberg, last week, and I trailed him to here. We got all the others with him, but he got away. I don't want any of your people here to get hurt, if there's any shooting. I figure the best time to take him is out on the trail, but he don't usually leave a place, till after he's already robbed it, so I thought I'd talk to you before that happens."

"I appreciate that young fella. Oh, my name's Vic, Victor Hopkins.

Now what are we gonna do to protect the town and town's money? I feel that you may be right about taking them outside of town. I'll go to the bank and tell them not to resist, then maybe we can save some lives."

Poe, "You might want to let them outlaws know you'll be out of town for a while, so they'll think it's safe to go ahead and rob the bank. That way, they won't do what he did in Ellensberg."

Vic, "And what was that?"

"Two of them went a little ways out of town and shot a farmer, so his boy would have to come into town to tell the sheriff, and as soon as the sheriff left town—"

Vic interrupts him, "Yeah, I get it that's when they rob the bank, very cleaver. You're right, if I sorta let them know I won't be here, then no one else gets hurt."

Poe, "Exactly. I already told the bartender I was looking for him, so I'll go and tell him that you just left town to go to see about a a—"

Vic, "A family squabble about something, you know, a man a beatin' his wife er somethin like that. Yeah, I'll say I had to go out to the Johnson place, ol' man Johnson and his woman are always threating to kill one another, and everybody in town knows it, so it won't seem like a put on. Only, ain't it a bit risky for you to tell him? You're a newcomer here. They're gonna wonder how come you know'd that."

"Yeah, I was going to try to join up with them."

Vic, "Do what?"

Poe, "Not really join them, just tell 'em that. I was going to say Mr. Moss, I heard you was the best bank robber in the whole West and I want to learn bank robbin' from the best."

Vic, "You think he'll buy that?"

Poe, "He might, because he hasn't even come close to being

110

caught and I figure he's pretty convinced, he can't be, so if I massage his ego a bit, he might want to pass on his expertise at bank robbing to someone else like a young up and comer in the outlaw business."

Vic, "Someone like you?"

Poe, "Right!"

"Sounds too risky to me," said Vic.

Poe, "It's either that or try to gun 'em in the cantina, or wait till he does what he did in Ellensberg."

"When you put it that way young fella, I guess we don't have much choice. You need an outlaw name like Texas Red, er the Missouri Kid er something like that, you know outlaws always give themselves a ridicules name, for some reason. Better yet, I'll have a poster printed up with your picture on it, and a crime er two, like wanted for bank robbery, and rape, er stagecoach hold up."

"That's it. I'll be the Kansas Kid, wanted for two, no three stagecoach hold ups, in Kansas and word is I'm heading for Mexico, so naturally I'd be going through Texas to get there."

"Perfect! I'll go to the newspaper office and get the poster printed up."

Poe, "And Sheriff, please make sure they only print one copy. I'd hate to try to explain a circular with my picture on it to a lawman that doesn't know it's not real."

Vic, "Right, only one copy." An hour later Poe had a circular with his name and likeness on it.

"Now, if I can convince Mr. Moss I'm an outlaw. Wish me luck."

Poe was just coming through the doors of the cantina when two of Clinton's new gang were on their way out and bumped into him. "Move boy."

Poe drew his pistol, pointed it at the man and said, "Hold on there mister."

The two men froze in place, and said, "What's this all about boy?"

Poe, "First off asshole, I ain't no boy, and you should watch who you're bumpin' into, I'm the Kansas Kid and I've shot fellas for bumpin' me, so if'n you don't want a get shot you better apologize."

The cantina at once was silent as a church, "Hold on there, son," said Clinton."

"I ain't yer son mister. I ain't got no pa on account of I killed him last time he whipped me. So are you gonna apologize, er do I shoot you?

Calvin, "I'm sorry kid. I didn't mean no harm, sa sorry, OK?"

Poe holstered his six-gun, and went to the bar, "WHISKEY, I want a whiskey right now, and slammed a dollar on the bar."

"Here kid," said the barkeep, pouring a shot, and then nodded to Clinton that this was the man that had asked for him earlier.

Clinton, "So you're the Kansas Kid, are you? I never heard tell of you before, I wonder why that is?"

Poe, "Probably 'cause I ain't been an outlaw long as you Mr. Moss."

"How do you know who I am?"

"Oh hell, Mr. Moss, where I come from, everybody knows about the great Clinton Moss, greatest hold up man in the whole entire West; yes sir, everybody knows about you."

Clinton, "And, where is it that you're from?"

"Oh, I doubt if you ever heared of it afore."

"Try me," said Clinton.

Poe, OK, you ever hear of Chiggersville, Kansas, it's up in Northern Kansas."

Clinton, "No, I can't say I have."

Poe, "See, I told you."

Clinton, "You got a poster on you kid?"

"I got this one, and produces the circular from his hat, this is the only one I didn't tear up. I see a poster with my picture on it I usually take it down and tear it up or burn it."

Clinton reads the poster. 'Wanted for three stage robberies, The Kansas Kid, Three-hundred-dollar reward.'

"The reward will get bigger, soon as I rob a couple of big ol' banks. Yes sir, I'll be real famous then. You'll see," said Poe, trying to play the part of a real genuine desperado.

"How come you told the barkeep you were my friend?"

"Sorry about that Mr. Moss, but I really wanted to meet you. You're kinda my hero, and someday I'm gonna be almost as famous as you."

Clinton, "Is that a fact?"

Poe, "Well no, but maybe, someday."

Clinton motions for the two men that were leaving to stay. They walked back to their chairs and resumed drinking. *Whew! That was close thought Poe, they nearly left to go and cause a distraction.*

Clinton, "Come on over here to our table and I'll introduce you to my guys." The two of them walk over to the table where the others were seated. "Guys this is the Kansas Kid. Indicating the man to his left and moving around the table that there is Texas Jack Harkness, Zeke Roper, and Calvin Barrs."

Calvin, "Say wait a minute, didn't I see you just come out of the sheriff's office?"

Poe, "Yeah, so what?"

Calvin, "Why were you talking to the sheriff, kid?"

Poe, "I went in to his office to see if he had a poster on me, so's I know whether or not I had to shoot him, before I robbed the bank."

"Wait a minute kid, you're not robbing the bank."

Poe, "And why not?"

Clinton, "'Cause we're gonna rob it, that's why!"

Poe, "But you just can't Mr. Moss, that bank was gonna be my big payoff."

Clinton, "First off, don't call me Mister Moss, OK kid? My name's Clinton or Clint."

Poe, "Sure thing Mr. er I mean Clint."

Clint, "Let me get this straight kid you were gonna shoot the sheriff, so you can rob the bank is that it?"

"Pretty much," said Poe. "Why?"

"Because there's better ways to do it."

"Are you thinkin of cuttin' him in Clint," said Zeke.

Clint, "Maybe, why?"

"'Cause we don't know nothin' about him, is why," said Zeke.

"I don't know nothin' about any of you neither."

Texas Jack, "He's got a point there."

Clinton, "We do need to get the sheriff out of town so he won't be in the way."

"Oh, he's gone already," said Poe, "some little kid came in and said there was a fight betwixt his ma and pa and for the sheriff to come quick, and he left while I was in his office."

"Who was the kid?"

Poe, "I don't know who he was, just that he had to get out to the Johnson's farm before his folks killed each other.

"Hey barkeep, come over here."

The barman walks over to the table and asks, "You fellas want something else."

Clinton, "Yeah, what do you know about the Johnsons?"

"Not much, 'cept they fight like cats and dogs and all the time, trying to kill each other, I swear I don't know why them two people stay together. I reckin' they just love to fight with each other."

"How long's it take to get to their farm?"

Barkeep, "Oh, about a half hour, I reckin'."

"That's it then, come on boys that's our signal to leave. Kid you hold the horses, you two watch the people in the bank, and Calvin an me will clean out the safe. Let's go."

Per Sheriff Hopkins instructions, two thirds of the bank's money was squirreled away in another part of the bank under lock and key. So the town would not suffer a complete economic collapse, leaving a mere sixteen thousand dollars, to be robbed.

"Hey, what the hell's going on here there ain't but a few thousand dollars here?"

The bank teller, trying his best to look as convincing as possible, said, "Sorry sir, but the bulk of the bank's money went out on a stage last week to the home office in St Louis, this is all we got now. Please don't kill me; it isn't my fault, please I have a wife an kids."

Clint, "Hell with it, let's go!" The five men got on their horses and rode off out of town.

Ajax must of thought he was supposed to race the other horses and took off like a shot, "Whoa boy, settle down," said Poe trying to rein his horse in a little.

Clinton, "That's one fine horse you got there kid. Where'd you steal him?"

"I didn't, I bought him with the stage coach money. I didn't want to ride around on a stolen horse, especially since he's one of a kind, and real easy to spot."

"Yeah well, he's an outlaw horse now."

Poe, "I guess you're right about that, now I'll have to go to Mexico 'cause there ain't too many people would forget a horse like him."

"I reckin' not kid."

Sheriff Hopkins was on a ridge watching through his binoculars. *Good job kid, now don't get yourself caught, he said beneath his breath.* Then he turned to his ten-man posse and said, "Let's just keep within range of them, and trail them till I can figure out how to take them without getting that fool kid killed in the process."

Clint to Calvin, "Go up on that high ridge and watch our back trail, I don't want any posse closing on us without a warning."

Poe, "I'll go. My horse is faster than all of yours and I can ride back here and warn you a lot faster than he can on that nag he's riding."

"You better watch your mouth kid," said Calvin.

"You're right kid, you go." With that, Poe nudged Ajax and took off.

"I don't trust that kid," said Calvin.

"You don't have to," said Clint, "I'm the boss of this outfit and I say the kid's alright. You want to argue the point?"

Calvin, "No, I guess not."

Clint, "Then do like I say, and leave him be."

Poe could see the dust caused by ten horses, an knew he would have to report their appearance to Clint. So he took off at a gallop and within a few minutes, he was back with the outlaws. "Posse coming," said Poe.

"How many kid, asked Clint?"

"About ten or so, I figger."

"OK, let's split 'em up. Jack, me and the kid will take the south trail you two take the east trail and we'll meet up again in Amerilla in ten days. Let' ride."

"OK, boss," said Zeke, "we'll see you there."

Now, I'm only outnumbered two to one thought Poe, that's an improvement at least, now how do I separate each of them from each other. Perhaps when Jack comes to relieve me on watch, I can get the drop on him. Then wake Clint with a pistol. Sounds like it'll work when I say it to myself it sounds simple. Still if he draws on me I'll have to defend myself, and I won't have time to ensure I only wound him. I may have to kill him. Unless I could somehow disable them, Then Poe remembered something his mother had told him years before, that the substance called cascara, will cause almost immediate diarrhea. If they both had this condition, they would be hard pressed to do anything else. now how could he obtain some of that magic mixture. He wasn't sure if the next town would have some or not.

* * *

The Capture

Chapter 16

Poe had already decided to capture these two outlaws, before the others rejoined them, so it would be to his advantage to do so as soon as possible.

As soon as the three of them hit town, Poe said, "I got a hankering for some candy, and I want to get my horse some carrots, so I'm going to the general store, I'll see you fellas at the saloon."

"Sure thing kid," said Clinton. "we'll be having a cold one right over yonder." He was pointing to The Cactus Spike Saloon, in the little town of Cottonwood, Texas, just over the border of Oklahoma and Texas.

"Howdy, young fella. May I help you with something?"

"Yes sir, I want a little candy, some carrots, some beef jerky and some coffee, and do you have any cascara?"

"Well now, let me check on that, he returned a minute later with a sack of the substance, and said, "You know boy, that stuff causes a person to get the trots, don't you?"

"Yes sir, I know, I got a partner that's all stuffed up inside, and a doctor told him this stuff will make him go like crazy."

"That it will son, only don't give him too much, else he'll be in the privy for a long time."

"Yes sir, I'll be sure to tell him that, thank you. Then Poe said, "Oh, I also need some beans." Putting the goods in his saddle bags, all he had to do now was volunteer to cook dinner for the three of them and make certain he didn't eat when they did, or what they did.

Returning to the saloon Poe found Clinton and Texas Jack bellied up to the bar. "Howdy kid, you get you some candy?"

"Yes sir, Mr. Moss, er I mean Clint, I've always had a sweet tooth, and I also got some beans and coffee."

"You get any bacon, or sugar?"

Poe, "No, but I can go back and get some, if we need it."

Clint, "Have a drink first, kid."

Poe, "I'll have a beer; it's kinda hot for whiskey. We gonna get a room at the hotel er make camp outside of town?"

"Why you care, kid?"

Poe, "Oh, I don't reckin' I care er not, it's just that I don't want to look for a good campsite after dark, is all."

Clint, "You see Jack, that's why I like this kid, he's always thinkin'. I think we should get a room at the hotel."

"We gonna rob the bank here too, Clint?"

"No, I think we'll just rest up here for a spell; we'll leave for Amerilla tomorrow. This little bitty ol' town probably don't have enough money in it, to bother with, so we'll pass on this one. We can always rob the bank in Amerilla, or someplace bigger than here. Let's go to the hotel and get us a couple of rooms, one fer me and one fer you two."

Jack, "I hope you don't snore, kid."

Poe, "No, do you?

Jack, "Calvin always said I did, but he's a liar anyways, so I don't rightly know whether er not I do. But I figger, if I do, I don't snore loud 'nough to wake nobody up."

The following morning the three of them were riding from town, when Poe, noticing the sheriff watching them, and gave him a sly wink. The three men rode all day and were all tired and dusty, and ready for a respite.

Poe knew if he could manage to separate these two from their horses that capture would be a whole lot easier, than chasing them all over the countryside, even tho' Ajax could easily out distance either of the mounts they rode. Noticing Ajax again, Clint said, "Yeah kid, let me ride that horse of yours? That is really one fine animal."

Poe, I don't think that's a good idea, on account of Ajax don't really like nobody 'cept me."

"Hell kid, I used to break horses, and I'm a better than average rider, so I don't figger that horse of yours is anything that special, that can't nobody ride him. Climb down."

"OK, but when he throws you off don't complain to me." Poe stopped Ajax and got down, and waited for the show. Clint walked over and grabbed the reins and climbed aboard. Ajax just stood there not moving at all.

Then Clint said, "See kid, he knows who's boss." As tho' Ajax understood this, he reared up and began to buck like he was trying to throw off the rider saddle and all. A few seconds later, Clinton picking himself up out of the dirt and said, "I know, I know you warned me. I was thinking of buying him from you, but I don't think he'd get me too far, seein' as how he don't like me none."

Poe, "He likes you well enough, but I'm the only one that he lets ride him. An Indian stole him once and he liked to broke his neck trying to ride off with him. My horse launched him like a rocket. So I reckin' you could say he's a one-man horse."

"I guess so," said Clint. "Seein' as how it's nearly sundown, let's make camp over there by that clump of trees. Poe, can you cook?"

Poe, "Kinda, a little, I guess. Ain't much problem fixin' bacon and beans, lessin' you want I should put a lot of spices and chilies an such in with 'em. Come to think on it, I thought I saw some wild onions back down the trail a ways, I could ride back and pick a passel of them, and put 'em in it."

Clint, "You do that kid, only don't take too long, I'm getting' hungry just thinkin 'bout it."

Poe, "I'll hurry, be back in a flash." Having said that, Poe climbed up on Ajax and rode off down the trail, knowing full well that the posse would see him, and he might get a chance to talk with the sheriff before dinner, and finalize their plans. Poe rode on Ajax, at a walk, searching for the onions. Upon finding them, got down and began to pick a few for the beans.

In a whisper, he heard, "Hey kid, you alright?" Turning around, he saw Sheriff Hopkins in the brush.

"Sheriff, You're taking quite a chance getting this close to those guys. They'll shoot you for sure, if they see you."

Vic, "They're not going to, I made sure that none of them followed you, before I got here. What's the plan?"

"Well Vic, "You ever hear of cascara?"

"Who's that, a Mexican bandit?"

Poe, "No, it's an herb that gives you the trots, and I'm cooking the chow tonight."

Vic, "That's a right smart idea kid, then when they're all out in the brush doing their business, we take 'em, right."

Poe, "Yeah, hopefully without nobody gettin' shot. I got to get back so they won't suspect nothing."

Vic, "You be careful kid." Poe rode back into camp with a bunch of wild onions and set about cooking up a large pot of bacon and beans, with onions some wild sage and enough cascara to give a whole platoon of outlaws the trots. All the men were seated having their meal, when Jack said, "Hey kid, these beans are really good; ain't you gonna eat?"

Poe, "Thanks, and yes I'm gonna eat after I feed my horse; he always eats before I do."

Clint, "He sure enough loves that horse."

Jack, "Can't blame him for that. I wouldn't mind havin' a horse like that, my own self."

Poe knew full well that now the trap was set, and intentionally untied the other two horses. Ajax, nipped one of them on the rump, causing it to bolt, followed by the other. Upon hearing their horses whinny, and then gallop away, the two remaining outlaws got up to chase them down. Within a few steps both men got the call of nature and went to the bushes to avoid soiling their britches.

Clint, "Damn you kid, what on earth did you put in them beans?"

Poe could not hear his remarks as Ajax and him were chasing the horses to ensure they would be out of reach of the two outlaws. Then, just like clockwork, the posse closed on their position. "Clinton Moss, you're under arrest. Your horses are gone and there's a ten-man posse surrounding your position, so you either give up, or get yourself shot to pieces, your choice."

Texas Jack, "I'm gonna kill that kid, if it's the last thing I do."

"Not before I do," said Clint, "to think I was suckered by a pup kid, I must be slipping. Well Jack, you wanna die here, or surrender and try to break jail later?"

Jack, "I ain't dying, till I get even with that damn kid." Then the posse began to fire and with so many gunshots, Clint knew that the sheriff was not bluffing about the number of guns facing them, and hollered, "HOLD YER FIRE! WE'RE QUITTIN'."

Within minutes both men were in handcuffs, and Poe was riding into camp with their horses. Clint, "That was dirty trick you played on us kid, and I ain't about to forget it."

Jack, "You little bastard, whenever I get out of jail, I'm gonna come looking for you, and fill you so full of holes, you'll look like a sieve."

Poe, "By the time they let fellas like you out of prison, I'll be an old man, and won't care how I die. But that won't be for a long, long time."

With two guards on each man, on either side of their particular bush, it was a full hour before the posse could even leave for town.

Sheriff Hopkins, "You two fellas best be finishing your business pretty soon, 'cause we're leaving for town in five minutes."

Jack, "You can't mean that; what if'n we ain't done yet?"

Vic, "Can't be helped? We all of us got better things to do than sit out here a waitin on you two, so pull up your britches and let's get a move on."

One of the posse men, "Looks like they both got A MOVE ON! Ha, ha, ha, ha," and all the men began laughing at this.

Feeling dejected, humiliated, and downright embarrassed, the infamous Clinton Moss, and Texas Jack Harkness were seething with anger when they saw Poe.

"I'm going to get you for this kid, if it's the last thing I ever do," said Clint.

"That goes double for me," said Jack. The men in the posse took turns telling jokes about the men's embarrassing condition as they rode toward town, bringing both men's demeanor to a boiling point. As soon as they disembarked from their horses, both men tried to outmuscle their captors, so they could reach Poe, but were unsuccessful in their attempt.

"I swear to God kid, I'm going to kill you for this," hollered Jack.

Once securely locked inside the jail, Sheriff Hopkins began to question Clinton as to the whereabouts of the other men involved in the robbery.

Vic, "Now then Mr. Moss, I don't suppose you'd like to tell me the whereabouts of your compatriots, I know for a fact there were four of you."

Clint, "You go to hell Sheriff! I ain't gonna tell you a damn thing, in fact, when them boys figger out I got captured, and that their share of the money is back in the bank, they'll be madder than a boiled owl. And, I'm positive that after they kill you, they'll burn this town of yours to the ground. So you better sleep with one eye open."

"Thanks for the advice, I'll do that," said Vic.

A Lone Kid From Texas   T. J. Rowdy

* * *

Horse Ranch

Chapter 17

Getting Ajax on the train the second time was much easier than the first, plus Poe gave him two carrots on the trip back home. "Easy big fella," said Poe, "you done this before, we'll be home in no time."

When the train pulled into the station, Poe was greeted by so many people he felt a little like a dignitary. Lisa came over and gave him a big kiss, and said how much she had missed him, some of the ranchers and farmers Poe had never met before came over to shake his hand and say how glad they all were that he had succeeded in getting back the town's money.

"It weren't all my doin', I was just one of the posse," and tried to play down his personal involvement. But most of the folks in town were going to consider him a hero, whether he liked it or not. When the bounty money came, it was way more than Poe had expected, and attached was a note from Sheriff Hopkins to Sheriff Higgins, saying that since it had been Poe's idea for the tainted meal that caused their capture, that he deserved every penny of it.

Bert, "Well boy, it looks like you might just have enough money to buy that land behind my place, with enough left over to get Ajax a lady friend, and, it didn't take no time at all. Not only that, but I want you to be best man at my wedding."

Poe, "You mean you and Alice?"

"That's right, two weeks from Saturday."

Poe, "What about your brother? He should be your best man."

"Nonsense, he's my brother, sure enough, and I love him, but if it wasn't for you, Alice an me woulda never met in the first place. So you're it, unless you don't want to."

Poe, "No sir, I'd be honored."

Bert, "Good, then it's settled. And, speaking about my brother, he's bringing another Appaloosa with him, to start our horse ranch. He said she might even be a better horse than ol' Ajax there."

Poe, "I doubt that, but then again, I ain't seen her yet."

Bert, "One more thing, Farley and me been talking and we both decided that you would make a right fine Deputy Sheriff for our little town. What you think about that?"

Poe, "Well I don't know what to say, 'cept thank you. But what about my job at the freight office? I can't be a deputy and a freighter too."

"Well since Beau needs something to do sides his schoolin', and so he won't have time to get into trouble, I'm giving him the job of loading the wagons. Alice an me talked it over and we figured it would be good for him. Besides, a hard day's work is just what that boy's needing, and he'll have some spending money."

Poe, "Oh, about Alice."

Bert, "I know all about it son. Alice already told me what happened at her place, and said how she sorta goaded you into it, in the first place, on account of her being so lonely and you feeling beholdin' to her for patching you up, and, I don't feel no different about either of you. So let's just let that incident go, and we don't never need to mention it again, OK?"

"Sure Bert."

"Now then, how's about you and Lisa comein' to supper at my place tonight? Alice said she was going to fix up something special for supper as soon as you got back, and you're back. So how about it?"

Poe, "How can I refuse, we'll be there. I'll go tell Lisa and get me a drink, and try to digest all this good news. I'm feeling kinda overwhelmed here."

Bert, "Oh and Poe, I hope you don't take no offense at my calling you son, because I know I ain't your pa, but I can't begin to tell you how proud I am to know you, and I couldn't be prouder if I was your real pa."

Poe, "Again, I just don't have the words to express my gratitude to you for all you've done for me, and you can call me son, as long as you've a mind to."

Bert, "Oh, you better go to Farley's office, before you have anything to drink, so he can swear you in proper."

Poe, "You bet, I'll do that right now."

[At Sheriff Farley's office] "Do you, Poe Dievers, solemnly swear to uphold the laws of the state of Kansas and the town of Ellensberg, to the best of your ability, say I do."

Poe, "I certainly do."

Farley, "Here's your badge and welcome to the right side of the law. I'm sure you'll do a right fine job."

A Lone Kid From Texas   T. J. Rowdy

* * *

Deputy Poe

Chapter 18

Poe wasn't at all sure how he felt about being an official lawman. It was definitely better than being an outlaw. But just the fact that he would be tied to a permanent place, a permanent position, and that some of the people he would come in contact with, were not all fond of lawmen, they were not outlaws, just not regular folks.

People that had lived out on the prairie all their lives and had little or no use for lawmen or the law, and weren't about to change their minds about them any time soon. Most of the farmers, and ranchers, would see and or talk to a sheriff, or deputy, on the rare occasions that they came to town for supplies. But then, there were the buffalo hunters, mountain men, and some, but not all, bounty hunters, that if asked would say that they had no need what so ever of a lawman. It was these isolated individuals, that oft times caused lawmen the most problems.

Hank Carstairs was one such person. Hank had lived all his life in the mountains, trapping game for a living. In his thirty odd years of living in the mountains, he had fought with and killed literally dozens of men, mostly Indians, but Whiteman as well. Because of his immense size, six feet eight inches tall, and somewhere around three to four hundred pounds, he was a giant compared to most, if not all the other men he had ever come into contact with, a surely disposition, and no manners to speak of. He was used to having his own way, most of, if not all of the time, with little or no regard for anyone else's feelings. Why he had decided to come to Ellensberg in the first place, was anybody's guess. But, the fact that he was here, his immense size, and disagreeable nature gave both Sheriff Farley and Poe reason for concern.

Poe saw him for the first time in the saloon, drinking whiskey. Poe noticed that everyone else in the place had given him a wide berth. Hank was alone on one end of the bar, and everyone else at the other. Poe knew without question that once this monster got inebriated that he and Farley together would have a tough time to get him to do anything he didn't want to do, like going to jail, or even being arrested. So far, all the big man did was to insult everyone he had talked to, but that was not against the law. Unfortunately, the more he drank, the worse his demeanor got, and both Poe and Farley knew it was only a matter of time before he did something unlawful.

Then it happened. Lisa came down the stairs looking beautiful as always and got within arm's reach of him, and was grabbed roughly by the arm and forcibly seated next to him.

Lisa, "Hey now mister, I ain't no side of beef. I'm a lady; you let go of me!"

Hank, "You're pretty, you should have a drink with me. I'll show you what a real man can do," he said, still holding her firmly in his grip with one hand and drinking with the other.

"I said to turn loose of me; you're hurting my arm."

Poe's blood pressure went up a few points, right then and there. Poe, "Hey there mister, the lady said to turn her loose, so I suggest you do that!"

"Who the hell are you anyway?" said Hank.

Poe, "I'm the Deputy Sheriff here and we don't treat our women folk like that, so let her go!"

"What if I don't want to do that, what you think you're going to do about it?" Hank rose to his full height and glared at Poe.

Poe, "Well now big fella, I'm not going to fist fight with you, but I might shoot you, so like I said, turn her loose now!" With that said, Poe pulled his pistol and cocked the hammer. Seeing the deputy ready to fire his weapon, the big man let go.

"I wasn't gonna hurt her none, I just wanted someone to drink with, is all," said Hank.

Poe, "You ever think to ask her?"

"ASK, I don't reckin' I ever asked no one for nothin' in my life."

Poe, trying to be diplomatic said, "You should try it, at least once. They say that you can catch more flies with honey than you can with vinegar."

"What the hell does that mean?" asked Hank.

Poe, "It means we have laws in this town, just like every other town, and you break the law, you go to jail. That's what it means, and, it sometimes works out that if you're nice to folks, they'll be nice to you. Not everybody mind you, but a lot of folks feel that way. It's a saying from the bible about do unto others as you would have others do unto you. You understand?"

Hank, "I think so."

Poe, "Good, that's a start now how about you coming with me and we'll see if maybe we can get you some work to do."

"Why do I need work to do?"

"Because that's what civilized folks do, we work, we get money for our work, and then we buy things that we need, like when you sold your furs. That was part of your job, first you trap them, then you have to skin them, and then you sell them. Right?"

"Yeah, I reckin'. You want I should go and set my traps."

Poe, "No, instead of setting traps, you'll be looking for work, then when you find some work, you do whatever you do at your job. Tell you what, let's go to the blacksmith's shop, maybe he can use you."

The blacksmith's name was Ollie Gunderson, a big Swedish fella that had lived and worked in Ellensberg for several years and was regarded by all those that knew him as an amiable fella and an excellent blacksmith.

"Howdy Ollie, how are you today?" asked Poe.

"I yam how you say fine, a hairy frog yah."

Poe, "That's fine as frog's hair Ollie, frog's hair or a hairy frog, what it the difference? Never mind about that, you need any help around here?"

"Yah, I need a team of horses to pull that vagon into here so I can fix it, but I'm not having the horses for pulling it. So dere it sits. I can't bring da forge to da vagon. I must take da vagon to da forge, so for now I'm how you say stchuck in da mud."

Then, as if he had actually been asked to, Hank picked up the yoke and began to pull the wagon inside toward the forge.

Ollie, "I'm not believing what I am seeing, I don't tink."

Poe, "Strong, ain't he?"

Ollie, "He is hired, there is much I can do with a human horse, yah."

Poe, "Thanks Ollie. I'm sure with you teaching him, he'll turn out to be a right good blacksmith."

Ollie, "Yah, I tink maybe you be right."

Poe left Hank with Ollie feeling as tho' he had actually done something substantial, as a mere deputy. Instead of arresting Hank, he had helped to get him a job, possibly the only real job the big man had ever had. So it was a good thing and all around good public relations for the sheriff's office. Hank could learn to be civilized, and Ollie had, as he called him, a human horse and everybody wins.

Then Poe remembered the trail drive he had been on, which brought him to Ellensberg in the first place. It was again that time of year, and those same guys he had ridden trail with were going to be here in a matter of days. *I wonder what they'll think when they discover I'm a Deputy Sheriff. I hope I won't have to arrest any of them for anything. Oh well, that's just the way it goes sometimes.* He would cross that bridge when he came to it.

134

And, come to it, he did. Two days later, when the huge herd of cattle hit town, some four thousand head, and of course some, but not all of the men he had ridden with, plus some new men he had never seen before. Two of these were brothers Jasper and Jedidiah Armstead, two first time drovers from somewhere south of Waycross, and not the friendliest fellows a person could meet, nor the best drovers, but were hired on just the same, as he had been last year.

Poe looked around for some of the men that he knew when he pushed cows with them the year before. Then he saw Will Plunket and Mr. Waverly, the trail boss. "Hiya fellas, welcome back." said Poe.

Will Plunket, "Well, would you looky what we got here, a Deputy Sheriff. How'd you get to be a deputy anyway?"

Poe, "I guess they just caught me at the right time an I just said yes, is all."

"You ain't fixin' to arrest any of us, is you?"

Poe, "Not unless you give me reason to."

Will, "You mean to tell me that after all the times we rode together, if'n I was to bend a couple of yer rules, you'd put me in jail?"

Poe, "Well, I wouldn't do it for spite er nothing like that, but if you did something real ornery, yes I 'd have to. I'm the law here."

Will, "Well I'll be, you ride with a man show him the ropes and what do you get, jailed, I never in my life, woulda thought that my friend Poe Dievers would sink so low as to put his own friends in the calaboose."

Poe, "Now Will, aren't you exaggerating a mite. First off, I don't see you doing nothing that bad you would get jailed for in the first place. Second, I'm just a deputy, the sheriff does most of the arresting; I just help out. Thirdly, if you was to get in a scrape with the law, it might turn out that I'd be in a position to help you out better'n I would being a civilian."

Will, "I never figured on that, you may be right, having a deputy on my side could come in handy. Come on an let's all have a drink, Yehaw!"

Poe had only had a sip or two from his beer, when he heard, "Well, woulda look at this now, if it ain't down in the dirt Dievers."

Poe turned around to see the only trail hand he had ever gotten into a fist fight with. One Cephis Best, a cowboy with a less than agreeable nature, older than Poe by a few years, but pretty nearly the same size. "Howdy Cephis, have a drink," said Poe.

Cephis, "Is that a tin star I see in your shirt there? Are you the law here now, Dievers?"

Poe, "I'm a deputy; Farley's still the sheriff."

"Well that's OK, he can take you to the doc's, after I whip you again."

Poe, "There's no need for you to try and prove you're still an asshole. I'm sure everyone already knows it. But, I'm warning you ahead of time that if you start any trouble, I'll be ablieged to arrest you, so don't force me to."

Cephis, "Arrest me, horseshit. I whupped you last year and I'll whup you agin this year." With that he took a looping swing at Poe's head. Poe had been expecting this and ducked under his punch and buried his fist in his opponent's mid-section, followed by a left hook, which sent Cephis to the floor, with a bloody lip. Poe motioned for him to get up and resume the altercation. Cephis got to his feet scowling and charged at Poe in an attempt to tackle him, and to get on top to administer a beating, but Poe was not the same green kid he had been the year before. He sidestepped the charge and caught Cephis on the back of the head with a hard punch, sending him face first onto the floor again.

Working as a loader, Poe had put on twenty pounds of muscle in the last year, and was much more skilled at the art of self-defense. Seizing the moment, he threw three short jabs and a crushing right cross to Cephis' jaw, dropping him onto the floor a third time.

Poe, "Get up big mouth, I can do this all day."

"Hold on there you two!" said Sheriff Farley. Poe, what the hell's going on here?"

Poe, "Hiya Farley, me and my ol' buddy Cephis was just getting reacquainted, is all," putting his arm around the neck of Cephis, and then squeezing ever so slightly, "but we're all through now," squeezing again on the man's neck, "ain't we Cephis."

Cephis knew he had been whipped fair and square, and said, "Yeah, we're done."

Farley, "OK then, let's have no more of this, I like things peaceable, and I don't figure saloon brawling qualifies."

Poe, "Whatever you say, Farley."

While Poe was engaged talking to Sheriff Farley, he had not seen Hank come in to the bar behind him, and without any ado at all, came over to Poe, picked him up and set him on top of his shoulders and announced, "This man is my good friend and I want to buy him a drink." Everyone in the place stopped what they were doing and all took a large swallow from their glasses, and looked genuinely shocked at this.

Hank, "You need to put me down. I'll have a drink with you, only I can't from up here, so please put me down." With that, Hank gingerly lowered Poe back down to his feet.

Poe, "Mr. Waverly, this is my friend Hank Carstairs. Say howdy to the boys Hank."

"Hello," said Hank.

Mr. Waverly, "Well Poe, it looks like you did alright for yourself, did you ever find that special horse you were looking for?"

Poe, "Matter of fact, I did, and, he's the best damn horse you ever laid eyes on, and an Appaloosa to boot. Bert Thomson and me are going to start up a horse ranch, as soon as we can save up enough money. But enough about me. How was the trip up here? You boys have any trouble with the Indians?"

Waverly, "Not too much, a couple of small set-tos, nothing serious. Let's have another drink, I still got a lot o' dust to wash down."

Scraps

Chapter 19

Sheriff Farley informed Poe that as a deputy he would be required to sleep at the jail from time to time, but since they had no prisoners, and Poe's rent on his hotel room was paid till the end of the month, he was not ablieged to sleep there as yet. So, deputy Poe opted for his own room at the hotel. The bed was more comfortable, and he had paid for it with his own money, so he'd sleep there, till his rent was due again. *That's right, he said to himself, you can save some money on rent.*

On his way to get some breakfast, Poe noticed a stray dog following him. He had always wanted a dog, as a child, but had never had one. He stopped and reached down to pet it. "Hiya boy, I'll bet your hungry ain't ya?" He wasn't quite sure what breed of dog it was, as it looked to be a mixed breed of perhaps Collie and Shepard, and not the best looking dog he'd ever seen, but quite friendly. Upon reaching the cafe, he turned to tell the dog to stay, making a pushing motion with his hands, and the dog stopped his pursuit. "I tell you what pooch, if you're still here when I'm done with breakfast, maybe I can get you some scraps from the kitchen. Poe finished his meal and when he looked out the window there was the dog sitting patiently waiting just outside the door. *Well now, you have to go and ask the cook for some scraps, he told himself.* Getting some half eaten sausage, and eggs, and a few bits of bacon leftover from someone's meal, Poe fed them to his new canine friend. "I suppose now; you're going to follow me everywhere I go. I guess that's what I get for making friends with a stray. I suppose I should think up a name for you. I know, Scraps. Yeah I like that," patting his thigh, he said, "Here Scraps, come here." As tho' he had always been called that, the dog came right over and sat down in front of Poe and gave one short bark. Bark.

Poe, "OK boy, it's settled; your name is Scraps."

Poe was curious about Hank and his new job as a blacksmith, but he knew he should check with Sheriff Farley first. So, he headed off to the jail. Walking in Poe said, "Good morning Farley," followed by a bark.

Farley, "Did you arrest him, or did he come here to surrender voluntarily?

Poe, "Oh, you mean Scraps? No, we just sort of adopted each other. Say, I wonder if he can track bad men. Dogs have a great sense of smell. I mean he isn't a bona fide bloodhound or anything, but I'll bet he could, if he got the chance."

Farley, "Who knows? Maybe he can replace that Indian, and we could pay him in scraps. That would help our budget. Hey, I know, you could go out and arrest somebody, and let him escape, and see if he can track him down."

"Very funny, Sheriff."

Farley, "Well, we would know for sure, if he can, or not."

"If you don't have anything real important for me to do right now, I think I'm going to go to the blacksmith's and see how Hank's getting along, being a blacksmith," said Poe.

Farley, "That was a nice thing you did for him, and I wanted to say thank you for that."

"No problem, I figger he's just like everybody else, 'cept bigger, and he needs to be around regular folks, to get used to them. I'm pretty sure he's been up in them mountains all his life. See ya later, Sheriff."

"See ya, Deputy. Oh, by the way, [Starting to chuckle] if Deputy Scraps works out OK, you're going to be the one to swear him in, ha, ha, ha,"

Poe, "You're really on a roll this morning, Farley. See ya later."

When Poe arrived at Ollie's Blacksmith shop, Hank and Ollie were making horseshoes. "Morning boys. I see you guys are busy this morning. What are those, horse shoes?"

Ollie, "Yah Vatch dis," Handing Hank a solid metal bar. Hank took the bar and with his bare hands bent it into the shape of a horseshoe. "How aboot dat? He is strongest man I'm ever meeting in my life."

"Wow! Hank that's really something. You're going to have all the horse shoes you can sell."

"Now my friend, I show you, da right vay to make dem."

Hank, "OK."

Ollie, "I ust vanted to show Poe vhat you can do."

Poe, "I'm impressed."

Then Hank saw Scraps, clapped his hands and spread his hands apart, and to Poe's amazement, Scraps jumped into his open arms.

"You know this dog Hank?"

Hank, "No, but it doesn't matter; he knows I like him."

Poe, "How does he know?"

Hank, "He is an animal, and animals have always liked me. I don't know why, they just do."

Poe, "Do you think he can learn to track people?"

Hank, "Yes, if you teach him to."

Poe, "How would I go about that?"

Hank, "I'll show you, watch. Here boy." Scraps came over to the big man and Hank offered a sleeve to him. "Smell boy. Get a good whiff." Scraps sniffed at Hanks sleeve and then Hank said, "Give me ten minutes and then give him a sniff of my clothes, and he will come to find me. I will hide in the woods."

Poe, "OK, go hide." Ten minutes later Poe said, "Here boy," and with a small piece of Hanks shirt, offered it to the dog to sniff. Sniff, sniff.

Poe, "OK boy, go and find him." Scraps barked twice and took off towards the woods. Trying to keep up with Scraps the best he could, Poe followed the sound of the barking and a few minutes later found Scraps barking at a large tree. Reaching the tree, Poe looked up and low an behold, there was Hank. Climbing down Hank said, "See, I told you he could do it."

Poe, "Yeah, you certainly did. Amazing! I don't want to keep you guys from your work, so I'll be getting back to the office. Goodbye, Hank, bye Ollie."

Poe had just got to the office, but before he could go inside, a wagon coming around the corner like a freight train captured his attention. Driving like a madwoman was Laura Densby a widow screaming for the sheriff, "Sheriff Farley, Sheriff my boy he's gone, he's gone. I think maybe the Injuns got him."

Farley was out the door and trying his best to calm the hysterical woman down. Farley, "There, there, Miz Densby, calm down and tell me what exactly happened."

"JA, JA, Joey wa, was going hunting, and so he took his rifle and headed off into the woods, and he didn't come back at all. That was yesterday, and he weren't there this morning neither. Oh my poor little boy; he's all I have. Whatever am I gonna do?"

"Now, now, Miz Densby, you calm yourself, and we'll get some men together and go out and find him. He can't of wandered that far away."

Laura, "But, what if'n the Injuns come an took him?"

"I don't think so, Miz Densby, but I tell you what; we'll get our Injun to look around out by your place, and then we'll know for sure."

"You, you have a Injun?"

Farley, "Well, he ain't exactly mine, so much as he's a friend of mine, and the whole town, really. Poe, would you go find our friend Tucinnae and ask him to come into town and see me?"

Poe, "Sure thing Farley. I'll go saddle up right now." Poe went to the livery and saddled Ajax and then rode out to the Indian camp to ask Tucinnae to help look for the lost boy.

Upon arriving at the widow's farm, Sheriff Farley asked Tucinnae if he would look around for any and all signs of any Indians. After a couple hours of tracking around the entire property, announced that it definitely was not Indians. "No sign, no Indians."

Farley, "See, Miz Densby, it weren't Indians, 'cause if'n it was, he'd a told us so, and he ain't never lied to me. He went in a logarithmic pattern from your barn to a half a mile out, and didn't see a single sign of Indians. But, he did, in fact, see your son's footprints north of here. So, we'll start the search for him there." With a dozen men searching, in a ever widening pattern, Farley knew that sooner or later they were bound to find something.

"Say Sheriff, what is a loggeremerick search pattern anyway?"

A logarithmic search pattern is just what we're doing, an ever widening circular search pattern, whereby we don't miss a single thing."

"Why didn't you just say, a circle?

"'Cause then, you wouldn't have learned anything."

"So how's come you're a sheriff, instead of a school teacher?

Farley, "Pay's better, and it's oft times more exciting, unlike today."

After an hour of searching the country side, Poe went back to the Densby's farm and asked Miz Densby for an article of clothing, belonging to the boy. Taking a shirt from the woman, he bent down and told Scraps to sniff it, and then he said, "Go and find him boy," and just like that, the dog took off in a northerly direction, with Poe running after him.

Now, when the boy was hunting for rabbits and squirrels, he wasn't expecting to come across a mountain lion, but he did. Fortunately for him, he saw the big cat, before it saw him, and he took off running towards a huge pile of boulders. Scrambling to the top of one, he then fell over into a large hole in between two more boulders, and was stuck about twenty feet down, in the dark. The cat was circling above him, trying to find a way in. Like any animal, mountain lions won't randomly jump into a dark place where there is no clear exit. An after several minutes of searching for a way in, the big cat finally gave up, and went away, in search of easier prey.

The boy was stuck between two large boulders, and was unable to free himself, and eventually got the call of nature, and was forced to relieve himself right where he was. The next day, it was getting hot and the aroma of urine was not a pleasant smell to endure, but once the wind shifted from East to South, the smell was picked up by Scraps' sensitive nose, and he could follow it easily. Upon finding the boulders where the boy was stuck, Scraps began to bark and the boy could hear him and responded, "Hey dog, I'm down here," he yelled! "Here! Here I am!"

Poe was out of breath by the time he got to where the dog was, and heard the boy's pleas. "Hey Joey, is that you?"

"Yeah, it's me. I'm stuck, and I can't move my legs."

Poe, "Don't you worry, we'll get you out of there as soon as we can. You just hold on a little longer, OK? Don't be scared, we'll get you out."

Once the others got to where the boy was, it was only a matter of lowering a rope down to him, and pulling him back up the same way he went down.

"Your ma's gonna be real glad to see you, boy," said Poe.

"Thanks mister, I got stuck and couldn't move at all."

144

Poe, "How'd you get like that in the first place?"

"A mountain lion was chasing me, and I barely got away from him."

Poe, "Well boy, you've had quite an adventure."

Joey, "Is that your dog?"

Poe, "Well sorta, he just kinda adopted me; do you want him?

"Do you mean; I can have him for my very own?"

Poe, "Sure, if it's OK with your ma."

Joey, "What's his name?"

"Oh, I call him Scraps, and he seems to like it."

Joey, "Hiya Scraps"; the dog licked the boy's face and they became instant friends.

* * *

Bad News, Bad Men

Chapter 20

Ben Morisey and Wiley Brant rode into Ellensberg looking for an easy mark; someone or someplace to rob, that would be easy and worth the risk.

Just as tho' they had wished for it, there it was, a very drunk cowboy staggering out the door of the saloon, and going into the alley to relieve himself in the ally, adjacent to the saloon. Without any ado whatsoever, Ben dismounted and clubbed the man with his six-gun, knocking him unconscious, and then began to rifle through his pockets. Twenty-two dollars and forty cents, "Hell, that ain't hardly worth robbin' him for," said Ben. "It'll get us a drink or two anyways. Let's go to the saloon."

The man Ben had clubbed was none other than Poe's old adversary, Cephis Best, and as luck would have it, Poe happened to be the one to find him lying in the dirt.

Poe, "What happened to you anyway?"

Cephis, "I don't really know. I was peein' and then everything went black. Damn, they took all my money, worthless sons a bitches."

Poe, "Take it easy. Maybe I can get your money back, once I figger out who it was that hit you. For now, let's get you to the doc's." Twenty minutes later, Poe was writing out a report of the incident in Sheriff Farley's office.

Farley, "Well, I see you didn't forget what I told you about the paper work; that's good. Did you ask around to see if anyone saw or heard anything?"

Poe, "Not yet. I figured getting him to the doc's was my first priority."

Farley, "Good thinking. One sure thing I can tell you about being a lawman, is that people that live and work here in town, usually aren't the ones that are responsible for any wrong doing. It's those that come here from somewhere else usually. So let's say you, Poe Dievers, are the sheriff. What's your next move?"

Poe, "Well, I guess I'd look around town for any new comers."

"Correct," said Farley. "So go and look, already. I'll sit right here and finish my coffee and you can be sheriff, for a bit. And of course, I'm available, if you need me. Go and see what you can find out."

Poe, "OK Farley, I'll be back in a while with my findings." With that, Poe decided to first go to the hotel to see if anyone new had checked into the hotel in the last couple of days. Upon entering the Sparrow's Nest Hotel, Poe saw the owner, right off. The owner and daytime desk clerk, was Hodge Peters.

"Mornin' Hodge."

"Howdy Poe, what can I do for the law today?"

Poe, "You can let me look at your register. I'm bettin' that the person or persons I'm tryin' to find, have checked in here in the last day or two."

Hodge, "This was Farley's idea, weren't it?"

Poe, "Not exactly; he just figured, and probably so, that anyone from out of town was a more likely suspect than folks that live here, is all."

Hodge, "Oh sure, all the most desperate outlaws come to my hotel to relax and rest up after a hard ride, running from the law. Fact, I'm thinking of changing the name to the Hotel Hideout. How'd you an Farley like that? Maybe I should run an ad in the paper. I can see it now. To outlaws everywhere, are you-uns tired of being chased all over the state of Kansas? Are you worn down to a nub? Is your horse fixin' to drop dead on you? If so, you can all find some

148

rest and relaxation at the new and improved Hideout Hotel."

Poe, "Now Hodge, "Aren't you exaggeratin' a mite? If I find out later, that the fellas I'm looking for were never here, then I'll make a special trip over here to formally apologize for my rude intrusion into your busy day. How'd that be?"

Hodge, "You don't need to, on account of there ain't been nobody check into my hotel fer three or four days."

Poe, "Thank you Mr. Peters, you've been a great help to law enforcement in our community."

Poe, "Well, I suppose the next stop will be the local watering hole and then the general store." Upon entering the saloon, Poe saw Ben and Wiley seated at a table drinking, and from the looks of them, this was not going to be a pleasant conversation. Never the less, Poe had a job to do, and do it, he would.

Poe walked over to their table and said, "Howdy fellas you're new in town? Where you hail from?"

Ben, "I don't see where that's any concern of yours, Deputy."

Poe, "Oh, but it is a concern of mine when people from outside our quaint little town get robbed and beaten."

Wiley, "We didn't beat nobody."

Poe, "Oh, excuse me; you just clubbed him over the head and robbed him, is all."

Ben, "Shut yer mouth, Wiley. We didn't rob nobody, so why don't you just go away and leave us be."

Poe knew these were the men he was after and baited them some more. Poe, "I tell you what, why don't we all go and find my old friend Cephis and you can apologize for clubbing him and give him back the money you stole, and buy him a drink and maybe we can forget the whole thing ever happened. How'd that be?"

Poe could tell by the look on Wiley's face that he was agreeing to this proposal. But Ben said, "I done told you Deputy, we didn't do nothing."

Poe decided he needed to run a bluff on them and said, "OK, you said you didn't do it. That will be easy enough to prove. Put all your money on the table."

Ben, "What for?"

"Well, "You see, it's like this; that guy's name is Cephis. I used to ride with him and some other fellas on a trail drive and of course at the end of said drive we'd all go in to town and see the elephant. And, we had this cook, name of Curly, that told all of us about this gal he knew that was really something special and said her name was Deliela. Ol' Cephis, he was all the time forgetting what her name was, so Curly told him to write her name on his money and then when we found her, he could remember. So that's just what he did. So, if none of your money don't have the name Deliela on it, you're in the clear. So please, put your money on the table."

Ben had never looked at the money he had takin that closely, so he knew they had been caught, and pretending to comply, reached beneath the table for his pocket and then upended the table onto Poe and pulled his six-gun, and fired two shots at the deputy before Hank, at the next table, picked up the five-foot-long table and smashed it onto Ben and Wiley, effectively disarming them both.

Hank shouted, "NOBODY GONNA HURT MY FRIEND."

Poe clamored to his feet and pulled his own pistol, and said, "You two are under arrest for robbery and assault." Sheriff Farley looked genuinely surprised to see Poe returning so soon and downright shocked to see he, in fact, had arrested two people.

Poe, "Case closed Sheriff, all I got to do now is the paper work."

"You got proof they did the deed?

"No proof of robbery and assault, but they did try to shoot me, which is assaulting an officer of the law, and resisting arrest. Which

I will not press charges for, if they return Cephis' money and plead guilty to robbery and assault."

Wiley, "I didn't touch thet feller. It were Ben, that hit him, not me."

"Shut up Wiley," said Ben.

"Well, now that you confessed to the assault, how about you give me my friend's money back, and perhaps I can persuade him to drop the robbery charge? Well how about it?"

"OK, here." Ben hands Poe the Twenty and change.

"Thank you, Mr. outlaw, I'm sure my friend will be glad to get his money back." Then Poe deliberately took the twenty and held it to the light and said, "Umm, he must have forgot to write on this one," and smiling, walked out the door.

Farley looking somewhat dismayed at this, asked, "What was he looking for?"

Wiley, "Some gal's name."

Ben, "For the last time Wiley, shut yer big fat pie hole!" Upon reentering the saloon, Poe found Cephis and walked over and handed him his money.

Cephis, "You found out who robbed me already, and got my money back? Was it them two fellers you was fixin' to shoot with, a while ago?"

Poe, "Yep, it was them. By the way, if you press charges you'll have to be here to testify."

"You mean come all the way back up here from Texas for a trial?"

Poe, "Yep, unless you'd rather sign a statement about what happened; then, you can go on back to Texas and they'll still git what's coming to them. But don't you worry none about them fellers getting off, on account of I arrested them for resisting arrest and shooting at me, so they'll get some jail time for that too."

Cephis, "Poe, I'm right sorry I ever fought with you in the first place, you're quite a fella, and I just want to shake your hand and tell you that if you ever need me for anything, I'll come a runnin'. Thank you."

Poe, "You're welcome, Cephis; let's have a drink." Five days later when the circuit judge came to town, the trial was held and both men got five years for assault, robbery, resisting arrest, and assault with a firearm.

Ben to Poe, "I won't be in here forever, and when I get out I'm coming to find you and kill you!"

Poe, "You know something big mouth, I'm pretty dang sure that you ain't gonna get no practice with a six-shooter behind bars. So you bring your rusty self, back here and we'll see how fast you are in five years." Ben knew what Poe had said was the truth and scowled at the thought.

Now as fate would have it, Clinton Moss and Texas Jack were supposed to have been delivered to the state prison in Texas, but due to overcrowded conditions, were sent to the state prison in Kansas instead. Both were wanted in both states, so the law figured this would do. But, a renegade band of Comanches, had torn up some of the tracks heading east, so the marshal in charge of them decided to take them north to Ellensberg, to put them on the east bound train from there. After a long dusty ride, they arrived in Ellensberg and went to Sheriff Farley's office to see if these prisoners could be jailed there, until the next train east.

Upon seeing Poe seated in Sheriff Farley's office, Clint and Jack flew into a rage, and both had to be pistol whipped to get them behind bars again.

Farley, "Well Deputy, it seems you've already made some lifelong enemies. That makes you an official lawman for sure. What did you do to those fellas to have them hate you so much?"

Poe, "Let's go eat some lunch, and I'll tell you all about it." As the two men ate lunch, Poe told the sheriff about using cascara to disable the outlaws. Farley laughed so hard he nearly fell out of his chair, and was still chuckling when they returned from lunch.

Farley, "I swear Poe, that has got to be the funniest story of capture I ever heared of. No wonder them fellas hate you so much. One good thing, neither of us has to leave town now. We can send our two prisoners with them two, and the four of them can go to the state prison together."

A Lone Kid From Texas   T. J. Rowdy

* * *

The Escape

Chapter 21

Upon witnessing the brutal treatment of Clinton and Jack, Ben Morisey decided to introduce himself and discuss plans on how to escape jail, and kill Poe. "I see you don' like that kid any more than I do."

Jack, "I hate that little bastard, and I'm gonna kill him, if'n it takes me the rest of my natural life to do it."

Ben, "Not if I kill him first, HE'S MINE, I TELL YOU!"

Clint, "Hold on there Jack, maybe these guys and us can get together, and all of us can take a piece of that damn kid, a little at a time. But, we got to get shed of the law first. Oh by the way my name's Ben Morisey; this here is Wiley Brant," reaching his hand through the bars to the other cell. Clinton Moss shakes Ben's hand and says, "This here is Texas Jack Harkness, and when you say it like that, it sounds even better."

"Yeah, a little piece at a time, make that little son of bitch suffer for a day or three."

"Yeah," said Jack, "we could all take a finger or two the first day and a ear the next, I think I like that idea better."

Ben, "I got me a idea of how we can get out of jail and maybe capture the kid too. Come a little closer. I'll lay it out for you." So with Wiley sleeping, the other three men began to plan their escape. "Now for this to work, we'll have to sacrifice somebody," whispering and pointing to the sleeping Wiley. "His big mouth, is the reason I got five years."

"I see," said Clint. "Well, if he's gotta go then, he's gotta go. When do we make our move?"

Ben, "Tonight, right after supper. I'll have him pretend to get sick and when the deputy takes him out to haul him to the doc's, I'll rush him. Chances are Wiley'll get shot, but I'll still be in a position to use him as a shield and get the deputy's pistol. Then, I'll let you two out, and we'll grab some horses and skedaddle out of town."

Clint, "Might work, but what if you wind up shooting the kid deputy?"

Jack, "Yeah, I want to torture him and I can't if'n he's dead."

"I'll try not to kill him right off, OK?"

Jack, "I reckin'." Unbeknownst to the outlaws, Poe had been invited to dinner at Sheriff Farley's and the marshal that had brought them there was gracious enough to volunteer to bring dinner to the prisoners. A half an hour had passed after eating, and Ben signaled to Wiley to fake illness. Ben began to holler for the deputy to come to the cell to help the sick man.

The marshal, "What's all the hollering about?"

Ben, "It's him. He's real sick and needs a doctor maybe he got poisoned er somethin'. You better get him out of here afore he throws up all over everywhere. I ain't sleeping in no vomity cell. Now, you got to get him out of here."

The marshal, "OK, OK, I'll take him to the doc's. Move back in the cell." Ben moved back to the wall of the cell and put one foot on the wall to push off from, so he could explode onto the man and hopefully drive him to the floor.

"Come on fella. I'll get you to the doc's; he'll fix you up," said the marshal as he put both hands on Wiley to help him to his feet. In an instant, Ben flew at the man and grabbed for his gun, and wrested it from his hand. But just like he had planned, the lawman got off a shot and it took the life of Wiley. Ben then pistol whipped the lawman and with the keys, released the others.

Jack, "What about that kid?"

Clint, "We'll get him later; let's ride." Finding horses tied to the hitching rails, the outlaws boarded the horses and were galloping out of town, within a minute. The marshal that Ben had clubbed with the six-gun died of a concussion, along with Wiley Brant.

Sheriff Farley, "DAMN, I hate to see people die for no reason. I wonder if he had any family. I sure ain't looking forward to explaining this one. We can't track them at night so tomorrow, come first light, I'll get up a posse and you go and find that Injun and ask him if he'll track for us, OK?"

"Sure thing, Farley." With Poe and six others, Sheriff Farley left town the next morning in pursuit of the three escaped outlaws. They had only ridden for a short time when Tucinnae announced that he had, in fact, picked up the trail and they were proceeding in the right direction.

"Good, 'cause I don't want to lose these guys. They're the only ones to ever escape my jail, and that kinda ruined my perfect record. Plus the fact, they killed another prisoner, and a U.S. Marshal in the process. So, I for one, will chase them into hell, if I have to. Let's keep after them. I think I want these guys more than anyone I ever wanted. The way I figure, they planned on sacrificing their friend just to get free. So they're despicable enough to do pretty near anything to keep from getting taken alive. So everybody, keep a sharp eye on any place that even resembles an ambush spot."

After two days of riding, the posse arrived at the little town of Gopherville, Kansas, which had a population of two hundred and five. But, thanks to the men they had been trailing, was now two hundred and two, as Ben, Clinton, and Texas Jack, had each shot an innocent bystander, after robbing the town's tiny bank, and taking no less than six horses with them, when they left. Each man now had an extra mount for when, the one they were riding, played out. This made Sheriff Farley even madder than before."

"Oh, I'm gonna get these guys if it's the last thing I ever do," said Farley.

Caught 'Em

Chapter 22

Sheriff Farley rode like a man possessed, hell bent on catching these men at all costs, pushing the posse to continue their pursuit almost without rest.

"Sheriff, you're gonna kill these horses, if you don't ease up," complained one of the men.

"Yeah Sheriff, like the one I'm riding," said another and stopped and dismounted. "See there Farley, my horse is lame, and we ain't no closer to them then we were before. Thanks a heap. I liked that horse." BAM! He shoots the animal.

"I'm sorry Skeeter, I know you did, but we can't let these guys get away. Why don't you ride double with Jed back to that last town we passed, after you rest his horse a bit. Everybody else climb down and we'll all take a few minutes and reassess our situation."

Poe, "Ajax ain't even close to lame. He's a mite tuckered, but a long ways from quitting. I could take the Injun with me and keep on 'em, and we'll leave signs. How'd that be?"

"That'd be fine son, we'll try to catch up to you by dark or a bit after, and thanks."

Tucinnae got up on Ajax, behind Poe and with his horse trailing behind, they left the rest of the posse and rode on. After they left Sheriff Farley said, "You know somethin boys, that kid's gonna make one hell of a lawman, someday."

Ben, Clinton, and Texas Jack, had broke jail and eluded the posse and were, to a man, feeling superior to lesser men who had been jailed and hanged. Clint, "I got to hand it to you, Ben, that was a right good plan you had to spring us from jail. Sorry about your friend."

Ben, "Like I said, his big mouth, like to got me five years, so to hell with him."

"Your idea to bring them extra horses proved to be a pretty good one. That thar posse's probably miles an miles away from us now," said Clinton, "You figure we can stop an make camp?"

Jack, "My horse is nearly all played out, so I'm gonna have to stop or I'll be a walking, and I don't plan on trying to outrun no posse on foot."

Ben, "Yeah, I reckin' we're far enough ahead of them to rest for a spell. Let's make camp over there in that clump of scrub oaks." With that, the three outlaws dismounted and began to make a night camp.

The stamina of Poe's Appaloosa, Ajax, was going to prove invaluable, as he got both Poe and Tucinnae within earshot of the three. Poe feeding Ajax an extra carrot and stroking his mane said, "You're one of a kind boy."

Tucinnae, "That is spirit horse, strong like buffalo, bad Whiteman no get away from spirit horse."

Poe, "Let's walk the horses to that next rise and see if we can spot their camp." Walkin' the horses to rest them and at the same time being quiet enough not to give away their position to the outlaws, they got close enough to listen to their conversation without fear of being discovered.

"Yep, that's them alright," whispered Poe. "Let's go back." The Indian and Poe crept quietly away from the outlaw camp and back over the hill, they came from. Poe to Tucinnae, "You think you can sneak down there and steal their horses while they're sleeping?"

"Tucinnae steal horses with them awake, they no see, no hear. Tucinnae steal many horse from Whiteman, many years."

"Perfect, then go on ahead and do it and, my friend, try; not to get shot."

"Tucinnae and Deputy Poe friend?"

Poe, "Of course we are."

"Tucinnae like Deputy Poe, too."

At four in the morning Jack got up to relieve himself an discovered that the horses were gone. "Wake up! GET UP, GET UP! THE HORSES ARE GONE!"

Ben, "What? Didn't you tie them?"

Jack, "A coarse I did. Probably Indians; ain't no Whiteman could sneak in here that quiet and steal 'em. Shit! Now we're stuck out here. We shoulda killed off every Indian there was, a long time ago."

Clint, "Maybe they just broke loose, and we'll find 'em come first light. Let's break camp and have some coffee and think on what we do next. Just don't panic, we'll be OK."

With the Indian on one hill and the deputy on the opposite hill facing the outlaws, as soon as the three men began to leave camp in search of their missing horses, Poe fired a shot into the air an announced that they were under arrest.

Jack, "That's him. That's that damn kid. Oh, how I hate that kid. I'm gonna kill you, kid," shouted Jack.

Poe, "Is that you, Jack? I got some good beans here you want some?"

Hearing this, Texas Jack popped his cork and charged up the hill in the direction of the Poe's voice, firing at the clumps of bushes where he thought Poe was. BAM BAM. "I'm gonna blow yer head off, kid." BAM BAM. Insane with rage and still coming up the hill towards Poe's position, Jack charged on, shouting, "I'm gonna kill you kid!" He was about twenty feet from the boulder where Poe was, when Poe stepped out an faced Jack. With his six-gun still holstered, he said, "Hiya, Jack, wanna dance?"

Jack moved his arm to bring his pistol to bear on Poe, and Poe shot him in the chest, dead center. POW! Jack fell face first in the dirt.

The posse, hearing the gunshot, whipped their horses to a gallop and closed on the sound.

"Good bye, Jack," said Clinton. "That wasn't too smart of you. But, we ain't done yet. I got a surprise for that posse, they won't be expecting. Watch this," as he produced three sticks of dynamite.

Ben, "Where'd you get them?"

Clint, "The last town we went through. I figured, these might come in handy. But we need to be somewhere where they can't see us, so let's get to cover."

Fifteen minutes later, the outlaws heard, "Clinton Moss, Ben Morisey, you're both under arrest. Throw down your guns and come out with your hands up. This is Sheriff Farley from Ellensberg."

Ben, "Ellensberg! You're kinda outta your jurisdiction ain't ya Sheriff?"

Farley, "Maybe so, but you're still under arrest, and you're both gonna hang. So, throw your guns out, last chance." The posse in a circle around the two hidden in the brush closed to within throwing distance, and out came a lit stick of dynamite.

"DYNAMITE! RUN FOR IT," shouted one of the posse men. A second later the air exploded with a huge bang, KABOOM! The concussion from the blast killed two of the posse and Sheriff Farley's horse and sent the sheriff flying. Both the outlaws stepped from cover, and cut loose with a barrage of gunfire aimed at their attackers. Ben and Clinton killed two more of the posse, leaving only Sheriff Farley, Poe, and Tucinnae. Farley got to his feet and drew his pistol and shot Ben Morisey in the gut, but not before Ben had fired at him. Ben's bullet hit Farley in the gut as well.

162

Poe had counted the shots from Clinton's six-gun and knew he was out of ammo, and walked straight up to him with a rifle in hand.

"You got more guts than brains kid," and raised his pistol at Poe and fired, click, nothing. Click, Click, still nothing. Poe clobbered the outlaw upside the head with the rifle butt knocking him unconscious. Then going to Sheriff Farley's side with a grief stricken face. He knelt down and gently cradled Farley's head in his hands.

Poe, "You hang on Sheriff, we'll get you to the doctor. You'll be OK."

Farley, "Not this time son, I'm going for the long ride. I want you to promise me something."

Poe, "Sure thing Sheriff, anything," said Poe.

"Promise me, you'll take my place as she she riff."

Poe, "You'll be OK. We just need to get you to the doc's, is all."

Poe started to lift him but Farley said, "Don't touch me kid, I'm through; ain't nothin' you or anybody else can do for me now, 'cept promise me yo, you'll take my, my pl place, cough, cough."

With tears welling up in Poe's eyes he said, "OK, Farley, I promise."

With that said, Sheriff Farley died. Out of anger and frustration, Poe went to Clinton and began to kick him savagely. "You sons of bitches killed a good man."

Tucinnae pulled him off Clint and said, "You say bad men hang, no kill now."

Seething, Poe relented and handcuffed Clinton and said, "Like he said [indicating Farley] you're under arrest. Matter of fact," said Poe, removing the cuffs, "you're going to bury them, here," throwing a shovel at him which he had retrieved from one of the saddle bags.

"All of them? cried Clinton."

Poe, "Yeah all of them, get to it, 'cept him," pointing to Farley. "I'm going to bury him, myself." Handing his rifle to the Indian, Poe said, "Watch him, if he tries anything, shoot him in the knee. I want him to hang."

Poe buried Sheriff Farley and said a prayer over the grave and then fell asleep beside it. Two and half hours later, Ajax nuzzled him awake. With it being only two to three hours before sunset the men decided to spend the night there, and take their prisoner back in the morning. "Cuff his hands behind him and tie him to him to a tree," said Poe, "and I'll cook up some grub."

The next morning, Poe and the Indian took Clinton Moss back to Ellensberg to hang.

The New Sheriff

Chapter 23

The whole town turned out to see Poe and Tucinnae return, with Clinton Moss, and at once noticed that their sheriff was not in attendance.

Poe thought to himself, *I might as well get this over with now.* In a loud and clear voice, he said, "I'm sorry to have to tell you all this but, that no good outlaw, Ben Morisey, killed Sheriff Farley." [groan from the crowd] "And, he asked me, before he died, to take his place as the new sheriff. So, that's what I'm going to do. Farley killed Morisey and I had to shoot Texas Jack. But, we still got Mr. Moss here to hang, and, you're all invited to the hangin'. Thank you." With that said, Poe rode off to the livery to bed down Ajax. "Feed him an extra ration of oats, if you would please," said Poe, "he earned it." Then he went to the saloon to try and get drunk enough to forget about the death of his friend and mentor. "Double shot and a beer," said Poe, when he entered the saloon. Anyone that knew Poe and had any reservations about him taking over as the new sheriff, knew better than to raise an objection at this particular time. Everyone in the place, with the exception of Lisa, left Poe to himself.

Lisa, "Come here, baby, I know how much you liked Sheriff Farley, but I for one, think you'll be a terrific sheriff, although I'm gonna worry more 'bout you now than ever."

The whole town again turned out for the hanging, and no one outwardly complained about having possibly the youngest sheriff in the territory, as Poe was both liked and respected by nearly everyone that knew him, and, the fact that Sheriff Farley had chosen him as his successor, made perfect sense. He was after all, the next in charge, and Farley had taught him whatever he needed to know.

Feeling the effects of the third hangover in his life, did not help his demeanor the following morning, when it was time for the hanging.

Since Clinton had already been tried, found guilty, and sentenced to hang. The only thing left undone was the hanging itself.

Walking the infamous Clinton Moss to the gallows, was a bit of a sadistic pleasure for the young sheriff. He was just sorry that his friend and mentor was not here to see it too. Clinton's legs became rubbery and had to be dragged the last several steps, all the while apologizing to Poe, the town, and anyone else he could think of right up until his neck snapped.

Then again in a loud and clear voice Poe said, "I don't like killing, I don't like having to hang anybody, but that's my job. That's the law, and that's the way it is, until the people that make the laws say different. I'd like to think I'm a fair man, and that everybody deserves a second chance. However, I'm not going to bend the rules for anyone. If anyone breaks the law they're going to jail. If anyone goes to jail, he gets a trial, and if he's found guilty, he hangs, period. If any of you folks has a problem you can't solve on your own, come an tell me, and I'll see what I can do to help. I'm not just the law, I'm also your friend, and as a friend, you can confide in me to be discreet, if it's something of a personal nature. I don't want to know your personal business unless it concerns upholding the law, or possibly breaking the law. I will do the best job I can, for you as, your new sheriff. If come election time, you folks want someone else, then go on and elect him. That's all I wanted to say."

To Poe's surprise, people began to applaud and continued clapping until he went back inside the office of sheriff. Somewhere between his second and third cup of coffee, it occurred to Poe that unlike Sheriff Farley he didn't have a deputy. So, his first official act as the new sheriff would be to find a suitable candidate for the position. But who? Then he remembered Hank, the giant trapper he had helped get work for, as a blacksmith. Was he smart enough to learn the law, was he willing to be a deputy? The only way to find out was to go and ask him. He would walk to the blacksmith's shop and talk to Hank.

"Goot morgan," said Ollie. "

"Good morning to you, too," said Poe. "Where's our huge friend today?"

"He's in bed. He has terrible pain in his head, and I'm stcharting to vorry a bit aboot him, yah."

"Has he seen the doc?"

Ollie, "He von't go to da doctor's. He says he vill be OK but I'm tinking, maybe not. You are his friend. Maybe you talk to him, yah?"

Poe, "Sure thing, Ollie. I'll go and see him right now." Knock knock.

"Go away Ollie, leave me be," said the huge man.

"It's me, Poe. You know, your friend, can I come in?"

"OK Poe, come in."

Poe, "You feeling a little under the weather there big fella?"

"I don't know what's wrong with me. I have this pain in my head."

Poe, "Let me take you to the doctor, maybe he can fix you up."

"Will you really go with me, Poe?"

"Sure big guy, I'm your friend and that's what friend's do. Come on, let's go and see the doc." After nearly an hour of examining Hank, the doc said, "I can't be a hundred percent positive cause we don't know that much about it, but I think he's got a brain tumor, and it's causing his brain to swell. That's why he's getting headaches. It may even cause him to go crazy, and I'd hate to think what he'll do, if he just up and blows his top at someone for whatever reason. Cause as far as I can tell, he's only going to get worse, and the pain will cause him to do most anything. I'm sorry, but we just don't know that much about this kind of condition. I wish I knew more. I'm sorry, but he'll probably have to be put away somewhere. Somewhere where he can't hurt himself or others, and I really don't know how to tell him."

Poe, "I do. Doc, would drinking a lot of whiskey hurt him anymore than normal?"

"Well, let me think a minute. I don't think so, why?"

"'Cause I'm going to take him back."

Doc, "Back. Back where?"

Poe, "Back to the mountains where he came from, where he'll be away from other folks, and won't cause any problems."

"Why don't you take him to the sanitarium in Kansas City?"

"I could, but I think he'd feel really out of place there, he hasn't even been around regular folks for that long as it is. Besides, I don't think I could get him to go nowhere, he didn't want to, without threatening to shoot him, and I haven't the heart to do that. So, it's the mountains or nothing. I'll take him back up to the mountains, but I can't take him no where's else. I just wouldn't feel right about it. Doc, do you think you could explain his condition to him? I think he should know."

Doc, "Sure Sheriff, I can do that."

Poe to himself, *He called me sheriff, yeah, I'm the sheriff. I gotta get used to that.*

Doc, "Now Hank, I want you to listen to me very carefully. You're very sick, what I mean is your brain is sick. You have what's called a tumor, and it's causing you to have these headaches, and in time, it's probably going to kill you. You understand?"

Hank, "You say my brain is sick?"

Doc, "Well not sick, exactly. It's a condition that we don't know much about. But, I think you should go to the state sanitarium, and see if the folks there can help you. That's my advice. Anyway, I'm sorry I don't know what else to do to help you, Hank. I'm sorry."

With that said, the old doctor just looked dejected, and walked away.

Poe, "Hank, you want to go back to the mountains?"

"No, I want to stay here with you and Ollie and become a townsfolk."

Poe, "Townsfolk means everybody, not just you, Hank, anyway don't worry about that. We need to find you a place where you'll be safe."

"But, I'm not afraid of anybody, and no one's big enough to hurt me."

"Hank, you don't understand. When your brain condition worsens, you may become violent and hurt someone without meaning to. You see?"

Hank, "I think so. Do you want me to go back to the mountains, Poe?"

Trying not to let the single tear that was welling up in his eye, fall, Poe said, "Ye, yes, I d, do. I'll take you there myself. We can leave whenever you feel up to it."

Hank, looking very sad said, "You're my friend, Poe, and if you really want me to go, I'll go. We can leave anytime you say."

Poe, "Tell you what big fella, you rest up today, and tomorrow we'll leave for the mountains, OK?"

Hank, "OK." The following morning Hank on his horse and Poe on Ajax waved to the children playing in the street as they rode slowly out of town, heading north towards the mountains.

A Lone Kid From Texas   T. J. Rowdy

* * *

The Last Goodbye

Chapter 24

The two men rode in the direction of the high mountains for two days without much conversation. Hank had never been much of a talker, and Poe could not seem to think of a single thing to say, that seemed worth saying. His friend was going to die alone in the mountains, and probably in a lot of pain, and there wasn't one damn thing he could do to change that, other than what he was doing. After coming to the base of the high mountains, they became to climb, and continued until they were far away from any semblance of civilization. The air was fresh and clean. The water in the streams was clear and sweet, and overall, everything seemed quiet and peaceful. They set up a small camp, and then went deeper into the woods to find some game for dinner. After spotting a four-point buck coming out of the brush, in front of them, and running in the direction of the cliff to their right, the two men separated, each taking a direction to cut off the animal's retreat. A few minutes later, a single shot, and there stood Hank with his rifle in one hand and the deer slung over his huge shoulder, holding it by the hooves with the other. "I got it," said Hank, "we'll eat good tonight."

After gutting it, and cutting off some of the meat for the evening meal, they hung the carcass up in a tree for the night. "I'll get some more wood for the fire," said Poe, "I know it's going to be cold tonight. By the way Hank, how's your headache?"

Hank, "It's gone for now, maybe I just needed to be back up here again."

Poe knowing this was wishful thinking said, "Yeah, maybe you're right."

A mother squirrel, smelling the smoke from the camp fire, came down the tree to investigate, somewhat in a panic, thinking she would be hard pressed to move her family of five away from another fire. She had learned from the forest fire two years prior to check out any and all signs of smoke. But upon moving down the tree, she quickly discovered that the smoke was only in the upper reaches of the tree and not all over, like it had been before. In fact, this fire only seemed hot down here at the bottom, and the closer she got to the bottom of the tree, the yummier this fire smelled. It didn't even smell at all like the other fire. This fire smelled like something good to eat.

Then at the very bottom of the tree, she saw what looked to be a shorter tree with only two big branches and no leaves and it moved. Now, the tree was shorter still and at the end of one of the branches was a small white thing that from here smelled pretty darn good. She would get closer still. *Uh oh, here it comes, run.* Running a short ways and then stopping to look back she saw the white thing lying harmlessly on the ground. She moved closer and closer, *Quick grab it and run back up the tree.* This white thing is part of what smelled so yummy. It was food of some kind. She took another bite mmmm, that is yummy. *I think I'll go back down and see if there's more. The tree with no leaves is moving again, very slowly and it has another white thing only it's closer to the tree this time. No matter, I'll chance it. Got it, I'll take it back up the tree to the kids.* Her hungry youngsters loved these little white things and she loved them too.

Back down the tree and this time the tree had one of the white things right there at the very end of its branch, *careful a little closer, got it, Mmm!* The tree branch didn't even move and this is the biggest white thing yet. *Oh well, no time to waste, got hungry kids to feed. Uh, Oh, another smaller tree but this one's moving, better get back up into my tree.*

Poe, "Oh, I see you already found the biscuits, I was going to surprise you with those. The cook at the restaurant gave me a whole sack of them. He said they were day old and figured we might want some on the trail here." Upon seeing the squirrel, he said, "I see you made a friend."

"Shhhhsh, said Hank, "she's coming back." The mother squirrel having decided that feeding her family was worth any risk she was taking, and these white things were just too darn yummy to pass up, she would get as many as she possibly could. This time the big tree that didn't move had a giant white thing bigger than her head. She would take the whole thing back up into her tree one way or the other. She tried to get a firm grip on it, but it only broke into pieces. *Oh well, I guess I'll have to make several trips up and down to get it all, still this is better than foraging for a few acorns, and her family loves these white things* Then she decided that these were not trees after all, but men. But, not like the men that wore feathers and shot arrows at her trying to kill her. Somehow these men would rather provide yummy white things for her and her family to eat. She somehow wished she could learn the difference between them, but that was not for a mere squirrel to know.

The two men ate their biscuits, with some beans, and deer meat, drank coffee and prepared their bedrolls for the night, with little conversation. Poe knew in his heart of hearts that he would have to leave his friend before too long, but not tonight. Tonight, he would dream of a different time with a healthy Hank and him living in the mountains, and trapping every day for the rest of their lives, and drifted off to sleep.

At around three in the morning, the air erupted with the sound of whinnying horses and the growling of a huge, hungry black bear, heading straight for them. Hank and Poe were between the bear and the horses and there was no place to run. Poe grabbed his pistol and began firing BAM BAM BAM. The bear was still coming, and Poe was down to just two more shots.

Then, out of nowhere, Hank appeared and charged the bear with his bowie knife, stabbing it viciously, over and over again. The bear, in turn, tore huge chunks of flesh from Hank's arms, legs, and torso. The huge man hollered like a Comanche on fire, but continued to stab the beast with all the strength he could muster. The two of them were locked in fatal combat with each other. Which would get the upper hand, or the upper paw first, the man or the bear? Making certain his last two bullets would hit the bear and not his friend Poe fired BAM BAM, to the back of the bear's huge head. With his last ounce of strength, Hank managed to roll the huge animal off of him. The bear was dead, but in a short while, so was Hank. Hank knew he was dying, and asked Poe if he believed in

God.

Poe, "Yes I do," said Poe, "are you fixin' to talk to him?"

Hank, "I think so," said Hank, "I talked with the preacher man there in town and he said no matter what I'd done in the past, don't matter none, and that if I asked God for forgiveness for the things I done, I could still go to heaven. Is that true?"

Poe, "I believe so, my friend, that's why he sent his son to die on the cross, so that everyone could be forgiven. That's the reason he done that. So the people that believe in him could all meet up again in heaven, with God. Are you sorry for the men you killed?"

Hank, "Yeah, I am."

"And, the bad things you done?"

"Yes."

"And, God made the whole world and everything in it?"

"Yes."

Poe, "Then, my friend, I'll see you again, when it's my time to go and meet up with God."

"Poe."

"Yes Hank,"

"Thank you for being my friend."

Poe tearfully, "You're sure welcome. Thank you for being mine."

With that, Hank passed on to the big mountain in the sky, where all the other good trappers go.

Poe decided right there and then that he would skin this animal and take its hide back to town with him and keep it for the rest of his life, to make sure he never forgot his huge friend. Then he would bury Hank, in the woods high up in the mountains, he loved so much. With the bear skin on Hank's horse and the solemn look on Poe's face, no one in the town of Ellensberg, Kansas that day had the audacity to ask what had happened.

Only after he had downed a double shot of whiskey and rubbing his neck and shoulders, did Lisa say anything to the town's new sheriff.

"You gonna be OK, sweetie?" she inquired.

"Eventually," Poe said, "It's just going to take me a little bit of time. You know, he saved my life. The last thing that big galoot did, was save my life, can you imagine that? When we get married and have our own house, that bear skin is gonna lie on the front room floor. So every time I look at it, I'll remember Hank, and him savin' my life. I'm glad I got to know him a little bit, at least. First, Sheriff Farley gets killed, and now Hank. My becoming sheriff is costing me all my friends; I don't think that's right. Maybe, I shouldn't be the sheriff."

Lisa, "You shouldn't say such things. Here let me get you a beer and we'll sit and talk a bit. Did I hear you right? You said when we get married."

Poe, "Oh, yeah, I guess I did."

Lisa, "Oh Poe, that would make me the happiest girl in the world. Come on, let's go upstairs you can bring your beer with you."

In his mind, Poe was back in the mountains with Lisa and the two of them were walking along when Lisa said, "Look there Poe, is that a mountain lion?"

Poe, "No, it's too small to be a lion. I think it's a bobcat and it looks to have something in its mouth probably a rabbit." The bobcat ran out of sight and then turned and ran back and then Poe could see that it wasn't a rabbit at all, but a small terrier dog of some sort and it was somehow silent, being carried off by the cat, then he had the feeling he was being watched. Looking over his right shoulder, he saw another bobcat, bigger than the first one, and eyeing him as tho' he would be its next meal, rather it's next four or five meals.

This cat's gotta be crazy, if it thinks it can actually kill me. Hell, I'm at least four times its size. Then feeling it coming in range, Poe made a fist and tried to pop it in the snoot, but it moved out of the way.

Circling around behind him and then coming straight at him he swung his fist, whoosh and missed a couple of jabs with his left. Missed. Damn thing's fast; every time he swung at it all he could feel was a touch of fur. He wasn't getting any solid punches in, *then he thought my legs are longer and they're twice as strong, I'll feint with my left and catch him with a right foot to the head.*

Poe caught the bobcat aside the head, and knocked it ass over teakettle. POW! His right big toe was throbbing with excruciating pain. He sat up in bed and sucked air hard through his teeth. *What in the world have you just done to yourself? You idiot you just kicked the hell out of the wall next to your bed. Water, put your foot in some water.* Half hobbling, half limping he went to get some water and put some in the wash basin and submerged his foot; better, but a long ways from good. *Let's look at the damage.* His right big toe was the color of a radish, and his third toe was bleeding a little. *The one sure thing he couldn't do was scream, because if he did, he would have to explain that he injured himself in a dream. That was sure to make him a laughing stock of the whole town. Still, you'll have to explain this ugly looking toe somehow.* Grabbing the water pitcher, he purposely dropped it onto the floor and yelled "OWWWW!" The desk clerk hearing him came to investigate.

"You OK, Sheriff?"

Poe, "Yeah, I just dropped that pitcher of water on my foot, is all."

Desk clerk, "That must of smarted some?"

Poe, "Yeah, it did!" Now, could you go and get the doc for me, please?"

Desk clerk, "Sure thing, Mr. Dievers, I mean Sheriff."

The next thing Poe thought of was making a mental note to himself to remember to trim his toenails, the next time they get too long, as now it's going to be very painful indeed. Apparently he had jammed his toenail back into his toe when kicking the crap out of that damn bobcat. Man, if word of this ever got out, he'd never live it down.

When the old doc asked him what had happened, he merely answered "I'm not sure, I was only half awake and then I broke the pitcher." I guess I must have dropped it, in my sleep, and it landed on my toe."

Doc, "That's strange, 'cause it looks like you kicked something with it."

"Just give me something for the pain, and we'll let it go at that, OK, Doc?"

"Sure Poe, I couldn't tell anyone anyway because of doctor client confidentiality."

Poe, "Good. I accidently dropped a water pitcher on it. That's it, period."

Later when running the incident over in his memory, Poe figured that part of the reason for such a bizarre dream was the loss of his friend Hank, and that perhaps he should go to bed a little drunk, at least for the next few days or so. After all, he'd had hangovers before, and although they didn't feel the least bit good, at least, they were not as debilitating as kicking a solid wall with your bare foot. He would make a mental note to have a double shot, every night for the next week or so. And, to Hell with those people that say whiskey never did anything good for a person.

A Lone Kid From Texas   T. J. Rowdy

Twister

Chapter 25

It had been two weeks since the death of his friend, and Poe was back to sleeping without the help of an alcoholic beverage. The town was quiet and peaceful, and no one had broken any laws that he knew of. So, Sheriff Dievers, his new title, was somewhat bored at having to be idle and relaxed. He secretly wished for a little excitement, anything, a bar brawl, a bank robbery, or even a violent domestic dispute. Anything was better than just sitting in this office and staring at the circulars on the wall. He hadn't gotten around to finding a deputy, and if this continued quiet keeps up, there won't be any need for one. And, just like mother nature had heard him, she decided to help him out with a little something people named a tornado.

A farmer named Harvey Allison came tearing into town on his buckboard, hollering for the sheriff. "SHERIFF! SHERIFF! A twister's coming, a twister's coming!"

Racing to the wagon and trying to calm Harvey down Poe said, "Take it easy, Harvey, slow down and tell me where is it now?"

Harvey, it's just north of here, and it's a big un. You can probably see it from a rooftop." Going to the hotel and taking the back stairs to the roof, Poe saw it indeed. It was a huge column of swirling wind and debris coming straight for their tiny town. Not that the town was small, but compared to the size of this twister, it was. It looked to be two hundred feet high and twice that in width, at the top. It was a funnel of terror, ripping up everything in its path. Through binoculars, Poe saw chunks of houses, pieces of trees, an a very frightened cow, all of which were circling around and around, at an incredible speed. The people that saw it were all at once, coming to him thinking that he's the sheriff, he'll do something. "I'm just a man," said Poe, "I can't do anything to stop this. This is mother nature. All of you go home and get in your root cellar, if you got one, and, if you don't, go somewhere where you can find a deep gully, or trench. A cave deep inside a mountain would do, I'm sure. The important thing is not to panic. Try and keep your wits about you. And, for God's sake, hurry! And, make sure you got all of your family with you. Don't worry about your livestock. You can't save them, no how."

Ajax he thought, He would turn him loose and was sure he was fast enough to run away from this, and knew he would find his way back afterward.

"If you're looking for yer horse Sheriff, ain't no need, I already emptied out all the stalls, and every single animal in here, left outta here five minutes ago."

"You're a good man, Simon. Thank you." *Thinking that since the jail was made mostly of rock and brick, that it would be as safe a place, as any other.* So, Poe ran to the saloon to get Lisa, and anyone else that wanted to go. Upon entering the saloon, Poe saw Henry the barman going to the cellar of the building. "Hold it Henry!" said Poe, "I think you and everybody else down there should come with me to the jail. It's made of rock and I think we'll be safer there."

Henry, "Now that you mention it, Sheriff, you may be right. I'll get 'em."

Lisa, "Oh Poe, I'm so frightened. Are we going to be OK?"

Poe, "Sure Lisa, we'll be fine, I think, but I'm not ruling out prayer, as a possible solution. If any of you got any pull with the all mighty, now would be a good time to ask him for a little help. With everybody huddled together in the jail, they waited. With the sound of the tornado passing over them was deafening, they heard boards creaking as they were ripped from the places they had been nailed, and items blowing around in the winds and then being thrown into buildings, with a thunderous crash.

The onslaught continued for a few seconds and then everything was stock still, without a sound to be heard anywhere.

"Is it over?" someone asked.

Poe, "I think so. Everyone stay here. I'll go outside and check." Opening the door, Poe could hardly believe his eyes, the town of Ellensberg was now a huge pile of lumber, brick, and debris. Thank God, Poe had taken the people from the saloon to the jail. As the saloon was completely gone, as was the barbershop, part of the general store, half the livery, and several other buildings. The only ones that seemed to be unscathed were the jail, the bank, the blacksmith shop, and the church. This was going to take a lot of work, to get this place to even resemble a town again. But, as luck would have it, only three lives were lost, a woman and her two children, that had been caught by the Tornado at the outset, as they tried to outrun it.

Ajax led all the other horses back to the livery, after the event, and looked as tho' he had been running for a while, and was genuinely glad to see his human again. The reverend held a special midweek service to thank God they had survived one of mother nature's more deadly threats.

Reverend Snipes, "As bad as it was, it could have been worse, a lot worse. At least, you all have your lives. That my friends, is something we should all be very thankful for."

* * *

Cactus Mac

Chapter 26

A month had passed since the Tornado hit the town of Ellensberg, and nearly everyone that had previously owned a wooden structure, was now rebuilding with brick, and or rock. Thinking, and rightfully so, that if they ever encountered another twister like the one they just had, they would fare better with a more solidly built building.

Poe had not paid for a beer in the new saloon, aptly named The Twister, since it had been built. Actually, it was still in the process like several other buildings. All of those people that had gone to the jail with the sheriff, had sworn that they collectively would not allow him to pay for a single drink. This custom, as Poe called it, would wear off eventually, at least he hoped it would, as not paying his fair share, looked for the most part a bribe, at least to outsiders.

This was the comment from one surely individual by the name of Cactus Mac. Cactus Mac was an underhanded, evil minded, ex-Major General from the Union Army, dishonorably discharged for excessive cruelty. He was hated by everyone that had the displeasure of serving with him. Why he had decided to come and apparently plan on staying in their town, was anybody's guess. Unlike other outlaws, Cactus Mac was a loner, no entourage at all, probably because he was so hated by everyone he had ever had any dealings with. He did however, have money. How much, and where it had come from, no one knew, but it was rumored that his bank account was substantial. Just the fact that anyone as genuinely, mean, nasty, and disagreeable as this man, having money, well somehow, that just didn't seem right. But, as Sheriff Dievers explained to one and all. Having wealth was not against the law, nor was being a complete bastard. So, just give him a wide berth, and perhaps he'll grow tired of being here and move on.

Poe was, in fact, the sheriff, but he was still a newcomer to a lot of the folks that had lived there all their lives, and was still regarded as a newcomer, by many of them. So, when it came to needing information, about someone, or something of importance to the law, Poe would most times rely on his old friend and ex-boss Bert. When Poe found Bert at his warehouse, he was loading an outbound freight wagon, by himself.

Poe, "Howdy Bert. How come you're doing this by yourself?"

"Well Sheriff, I'll tell ya. Once upon a time, I had this kid that did this for me, and he was real good at it too. But, the town went and made him sheriff and now I'm breaking my back, doing it myself."

Poe, "Very funny Bert, here let me give you a hand."

"Thank you Sheriff, I surely do appreciate it." Bert almost never called Poe Sheriff and never twice in one day before.

Poe, "What's up Bert?"

Bert, "Well, now that you asked, I'll tell you. I'm doing this myself because there's no one to hire to help me." The two men loaded the wagon as they talked. Poe hadn't done any loading for over a month and he could tell right off that he wasn't quite as strong as he had been when he did this type of work every day. "Whew!" said Poe, as they loaded the last of the freight. "I must be a little out of shape."

Bert, "Or a lot. Let me ask you something, Sheriff?"

Poe, "OK now Bert, you know my name and that's the third time you called me Sheriff. What's going on?"

Bert, "Haven't you noticed that there aren't ANY DRIFTERS AROUND ANYMORE?"

Poe, "What do you mean?"

"Just what I said. I haven't been able to hire anyone to help me, because there isn't anyone available. I haven't even seen a stranger in over a month, no two or three cowboys a ridin' together,

184

no gamblers just passing through, no lone drifters looking for a bed for a night, nothing. Doesn't that seem a little strange to you, Sheriff?"

Poe, "Now that you put it that way, yes I suppose it does. You suppose?"

"Boy, you better do more than suppose! Something's going on out there, somewhere out of town. I don't know exactly what it could be, but I know for certain that something is definitely wrong. I've lived here for better'n thirty years and I ain't never seen the town this devoid of new people. I know the tornado probably scared some folks into not coming here, but that was quite a while ago, and this town isn't going to grow at all without new people coming here."

Poe, "Now that you mention it, I haven't seen any NEW folks at all, 'cept that Cactus Mac fella."

"Who'd you say?" asked Bert.

Poe, "Oh some nasty son of a bitch calls himself Cactus Mac. He's an ex-Union General, dishonorably discharged for being an asshole."

Bert, "Maybe he's the reason. How long's this Cactus Mac fella been here?"

Poe, "I don't know for sure, a month, maybe."

"That's just about the time all the newcomers started to disappear," said Bert.

Poe, "What do you mean, disappear?"

Bert, "Just what I said. I hired this young fella to do the loading, and he never showed up for work, and it wasn't 'cause he got drunk, or over slept, or went to jail. He never showed up period. He just up and disappeared. Twice that's happened. It might be just a coincidence, but I don't believe in them. I think he was snatched up by someone or something that needs a lot of bodies for something, like a army, or a work force. I could be wrong, but I'll bet you my month's pay, that something nefarious is going on outside of town, and so, Mr. Dievers Sheriff, you need to go and snoop around a bit and find out, and, thanks for the help with the wagon."

"You're welcome Bert, and thanks for your insight. I guess I'm still a little green in some ways."

"Anytime son. Go get 'em."

Poe decided that Bert was probably right about it being Cactus Mac. So, he would follow him around and see where that leads him. Ironically, after following Mac around at a distance, Poe wound up back at Bert's warehouse.

"You rent out wagons?" asked Mac.

"Occasionally," said Bert. "Why, you got some freight to haul somewhere?"

Mac, "None of yer business, what I'm using it for. You got a wagon to rent or ain't ya?"

Bert immediately detested this arrogant man and said, "No, I ain't got one available, now, but if'n you come back in a week or so, I might have one then."

"To hell with you then," said Mac, and walked away.

Poe heard this from around the corner of the warehouse, where he had been listening. "Charming fella, ain't he?" said Poe.

Bert, "Yeah, a real sweetheart, I'll bet he was raised by wolves. I'd keep a close eye on him, if I were you, boy, and, you be real careful. I wouldn't trust that S.O.B. as far as I could throw him."

"I'll be careful." Poe followed Cactus Mac for the better part of the day, but got no inkling of what if anything he was up to, and decided to go to dinner. He was only half way through his meal, when he looked up and saw Mac driving a wagon past the diner heading out of town. Poe, "Save this for me I'll be back later, thanks," and rushed to the livery to saddle Ajax.

Once saddled, Poe rode out of town, following the wagon tracks until he was sure of their direction and the topography of the landscape, and knew he would be able to find the trail again the following morning. Then he returned to the café to finish his supper.

The next morning, Poe saddled Ajax, and was on the trail following the wagon tracks in the direction he had gone the evening before. He would track the wagon and close in on Max's position as soon as he could determine the right course of action. The wagon tracks led to a small clearing in the foothills, that could only be seen form one direction on one particular rise of earth. This was the perfect place to hide an army or large building.

Poe tied Ajax to a clump of trees and crept ever so gingerly forward toward the partially finished building. Soon he heard the sound of picks and shovels and men working. Crack! "Get your lazy butt up and keep moving," said the man with the whip. Poe could see that this was some kind of work camp, full of slaves. These were men that were doing hard labor against their will. The man with the whip was Cactus Mac's second in command, a large man of Turkish decent named Yusef Bartouk, an escaped convict and murderer from his own country and nearly as mean as Mac himself. Poe could see several tons of dirt which had been dug, unearthed and piled up in a defensive perimeter surrounding what appeared to be an underground structure of some sort, made mostly of rock. As wheel barrels of dirt were coming out and loads of rock were going in. There were a couple of out buildings for supplies and a least three wagons that Poe could see from his vantage point. *What in the world was this guy up to? Poe wondered.*

Suddenly, Poe heard the unmistakable click of a forty-four being cocked for action. "Don't try it, you'll never make it," said a voice from behind him. Then a hand went to his side and removed his six-gun.

"Stand up mister". Poe complied. "Turn around slowly." Poe turned and saw a man holding a rifle and pointing it at his stomach.

Poe, "OK mister, don't shoot. I'm not going anywhere right this second."

"A lawman!" exclaimed the man, "I hit pay dirt! Nice an easy now lawman, down the hill, and don't do nothin' stupid, 'cause I'll be abliged to shoot you." Poe hadn't counted on being anybody's prisoner, but that was now the predicament he found himself in. Upon entering the underground dwelling, Poe came face to face with Cactus Mac.

"Sheriff, fancy meeting you here," said Mac. "We'll have to put you some place special. Yes sir, we're gonna get a lot of work outta you. Put 'em on him." Then a man in charge of the chains, began to attach a set of leg irons to Poe's ankles. Then he was handed a pick and told to dig. Five hours later, exhausted, Poe asked another prisoner, "What they were building?"

"Shhhhsh! Quiet," said the man. "They catch you talking you'll get the whip."

Whispering, Poe ventured, "What is this place?"

Another man answered, "Welcome to Hell."

Once it became dark, Ajax deduced that Poe must be in some sort of trouble, because he had never left him tied for that long without returning. So, he began to pull at the reins, tied to the brush. Within a minute or so he was free and started for home. The following morning, upon seeing Ajax in his stall and still saddled, Mr. Peters, the stableman, went to Bert's warehouse to find him. He knew that somehow Poe must be in trouble because Ajax had come back alone, and Bert was Poe's closest friend.

"What's up?" asked Bert.

Simon, "I think our new sheriff's in some kind of trouble."

Bert, "Why you say that?"

"Because his horse came back without him, and you know as well as I do, that that kid would never let that happen, if he could help it."

Bert, "You're right about that, he must be in some kind of trouble. I'll get some men together for a posse. Can you saddle my horse?"

"Sure thing."

Bert, "And, I'll tell whomever I can find, to help."

A Lone Kid From Texas   T. J. Rowdy

* * *

The Rescue

Chapter 27

Poe had been working like a Hebrew slave, since the wee hours of the morning, and it was, he figured, now around noon. The task masters had called a stop to the drudgery long enough to feed them, if the slop they dished out could be called food. It was usually a bowl of mush, or some sort of strange stew.

Poe knew Ajax would free himself and go back to the stable, because he was not only a smart animal, but he also only loosely tied him, in the event he could not return, like now. It was only a matter of time before someone discovered that the town's new sheriff was indeed missing. Poe hoped that his disappearance would be noticed sooner than later.

In the meantime, he had to try an devise a plan to free himself, and hopefully, some, if not all, of the others, but how? Everyone was chained at the ankles, and there were guards watching their every move. Who was this maniac, and what was he building? Then, he saw it a conglomeration of ancient torture devises, from the days of old, in merry old England, France, and Germany. He saw hundreds of feet of chain, saws, chopping machines, and blades for cutting flesh. This guy was insane for sure, a complete madman. Did he really plan to use these things on people? Apparently so.

Poe suddenly got a very sick feeling in the pit of his stomach, and prayed to God that someone was on the way to their rescue, perhaps Bert and some of the towns people. He could only hope that was the case, or he and his compatriots were in the worst possible place on earth, in the hands of a genuine madman.

Meanwhile, back in town, Bert and several others were forming up a posse to go and find their new sheriff. Bert, "I think we need to get that Indian to track for us. He knows Poe and Ajax's tracks better'n anyone."

Before the posse could leave town, no less than three U.S. Marshals rode up and asked who the town's sheriff was.

Bert, "His name is Poe Dievers but he isn't here at present. One of the marshals, "Where prey tell is he?"

"We'd like to know that ourselves Marshal. We were just fixin' to go out an look for him, and if I might be so bold, how come there's three of you, instead of just one?"

"We're after a really dangerous hombre that used to be a officer in the Union Army."

Bert, "You mean Cactus Mac?"

Marshal, "The very same. We're almost positive, he's behind the theft of a quarter of a million dollars' worth of army gold. The shipment was held up in a military fashion. This man's been arrested for murder three times, and every time the witnesses against him have died of mysterious causes. The gold shipment was one of the biggest the army ever had. There's three of us because we all three have a score to settle with that despicable gentleman. Only an experienced army officer could have pulled it off, and we think it's him."

Bert, "Now, it makes sense."

"What's that?"

"I think the man you're looking for is out there on the prairie, and has been snatching people for something, for quite a while now. He may have an army by now. Perhaps, not a willing army, but an army none the less. We were just getting up a posse to go and hunt him down, and you're more than welcome to join us."

"We'll do that. Thank you."

Deep beneath the hidden structure of Cactus Mac's hideout, was a sub-basement where only Mac, Yusef, and a select few were allowed access. This was the prayer chamber, an alter with an upside down cross, and all sorts of demonic paraphernalia. Macintosh Creedo A.K.A. Cactus Mac was a devil worshiper, a Satanist. His ultimate goal was to construct a demonic temple, complete with its own torture chamber, to sacrifice souls to the devil, his Master and God. He had robbed the army's gold for this one purpose, and by all accounts, was in fact, completely insane. Upon seeing this Poe decided right then and there, that come hell or high water, he would die before he would succumb to torture from this evil maniac.

True to form, Tucinnae tracked Poe and Ajax's trail to the madman's hideout.

"Look there," said one of the marshals, "it's the same thing we saw the last time we got this close."

Bert, "What do you mean?"

"Look," said the marshal, pointing to the graves outside the dirt mound. Some of the graves had crosses but were turned upside down in the dirt. "Yeah, it's him alright," said one of the other marshals. "I think we finally got him."

Surrounding the encampment with men from the posse, the leader of the marshals hollered for Cactus Mac to show himself. "Your surrounded. You haven't got a chance. Give yourself up and nobody needs to get hurt."

Before he could finish his statement the air was filled with gunfire. Men from the posse then began firing both pistols and shotguns, along with rifles. The inside of the perimeter was besieged by gunfire, and the men inside, were hard pressed to even return fire, once the posse opened up on them, with the amount of ammunition being expended by the posse.

The guards were beginning to throw their guns out and surrender. Shooting two of them, Mac screamed you're all a bunch of cowards, and retreated to his inner sanctum in the bowels of the unfinished building. Poe picked up a pistol from off the ground and used it to shoot the leg irons and free himself from the shackles and went to find a door to the chamber below. Finding the entrance, he moved as quiet as a cat, wanting to surprise Mac, if possible. Suddenly, Yusef jumped out at him with a large sword, but was a second late. Poe shot him in the face. BAM! Hearing the shot, Mac took up a defensive posture behind his pulpit with a sword in his hand and said, "So Sheriff, what do you say to a duel, my God against yours?" Poe's first thought was to shoot him. but this six-gun was out of bullets, so he said, "Why not. I'm not all that familiar with God's punishment of sick minded son a bitches like you, but I'm fairly certain he'll know where to send you, once I get you to him." Poe was not a swordsman but he still had youth and speed on his side. Plus, if push came to shove, he would almost bet that the good lord wanted this crazy asshole off the planet. Swishing the sword back and forth he waited for Cactus to charge. A second later and he did, with a furious attempt to skewer Poe with his sword.

Poe did a downward swipe with his own sword in a circle and then another circle and a thrust and much to his surprise, caught Mac on the arm with a poke.

"So," said Mac, "I see that you're not a stranger to the blade?"

"Wrong! I never had a lesson, but then, I work for the good guys," and saluted with the saber. Incensed at this kid's arrogance, Cactus Mac sliced back an forth trying to somehow dislodge Poe's saber. Parrying his sword with that of Mac's, Poe pushed forward then ducked just in time as the evil man's sword swiped the air above him. Then Mac tried to sidestep and thrust at Poe from a different angle. But, Poe countered this as well. Poe wanting to further psych out his opponent, he said, "Hey, I'm getting the hang of this, I think. Maybe I'll take a few lessons."

Hearing this, fueled Mac's hatred of this young upstart, and thrust at him with a determined stab. Poe had hoped he would try that very thing and sidestepped his lunge and swung his saber with all his might, and sliced Mac's neck, cutting his juggler vain.

When Poe emerged from the dungeon to see the marshals and the posse cuffing the remaining few bad guys, and giving water to the prisoners, Poe was asked, "Did you kill him."

Poe replied, "I sent him to see his boss, Beelsabub or whatever you call Satan. But, I'm sure God is going to have a chat with him first. Still holding the dueling saber, Poe said "Hey you fellas mind very much if I hang on to this thing?"

One of the marshals, "Be my guest."

Poe, "Thanks, I think I'll put it over my fireplace, whenever I get a house." Then Poe looked around and saw his friend Bert. "Hiya, Bert. You guys got here just in time. That lunatic was fixin' to torture us, and boy am I hungry. You bring any jerky with you?"

Bert, "Glad to see you, boy. Here," and hands Poe a piece of jerky, "Chew on that till we get you back to town."

"Thanks, Bert, and thanks for coming after me. I don't know if I'm all that cut out for being a lawman or not. I like a little excitement, same as anyone else, but this job is getting downright dangerous, and I think I'm going to quit while I'm ahead. Besides, I'm pretty sure I want to marry Lisa, and have a family, and I don't figure I have the right to have her worry over me, every time I leave town to chase down some outlaw. So, as soon as we get back I'm quitting. I'll stay on until the town gets someone to take my place, but as soon as they do, I'm going to get me some other line of work."

Bert, "You sure about that boy?"

Poe, "Yeah, I' m sure. I'm just a lone kid from Texas, and all I want from now on is to raise horses and kids. By the way, did you ever hear from your brother about a mare for Ajax?"

Bert, "Have I got a surprise for you. Actually, it's more of a surprise for him," pointing to Ajax.

Poe, "You mean, he found one?"

Bert, "You bet, and she's a real beauty, might be a better looking horse that him."

Poe, "She'd have to be one fine horse."

A Lone Kid From Texas   T. J. Rowdy

Bert, "She is, you wait and see."

The End

www.ingramcontent.com/pod-product-compliance
Lightning Source LLC
Chambersburg PA
CBHW072105170626
46813CB00004B/1470